BEYOND THE
COLORS OF DARKNESS

Borgo Press Books by BRIAN STABLEFORD

BEYOND THE COLORS OF DARKNESS

AND OTHER EXOTICA

by

Brian Stableford

THE BORGO PRESS

An Imprint of Wildside Press LLC

MMIX

CONTENTS

INTRODUCTION

Alexander Baumgarten, the fonder of modern aesthetics, disapproved on what he called "heterocosmic creativity": writing stories set in worlds unlike the one that we experience. He had already defined artistic work as "secondary creativity", thus representing it as a microcosmic imitation of the work of God, and—because he was a follower of Gottfried Leibniz and accepted the argument Leibniz had put forward in his *Theodicy*—he believed that God, being good, had made the best of all possible worlds. For a secondary creator to devise and work within worlds unlike the one God had made was, therefore, to work with inferior clay; true artists ought to do their level best—just as God had—to simulate the best of all possible worlds: the one in which they served as creatures.

Some people, even within his native Germany, found it hard to agree with Leibniz that the world in which we live is the best of all possible worlds; some found it all too easy to find evidence within it, not merely of shoddy workmanship, but of sheer stupidity or downright craziness. Voltaire, who wrote a long series of *contes philosophiques* designed to display (as the title of the first put it) "The World as it Is", parodied Leibniz as Doctor Pangloss, who met every incidence of dire misfortune and all evidence of the sheer vileness of everyday human depravity with the cheery reminder that "all is for the best in the best of all possible worlds". By and large, most people thereafter sided with Voltaire in considering that Leibniz had not, after all, solved the problem of evil by suggesting that the world was a mess because God had had such lousy materials and poor tools with which to work.

By the same token, many artists have abandoned Baumgarten's dictum that the best art is the most carefully representative; the subsequent history of the visual arts has been, in large measure, a story of the gradual abandonment of straightforward visual realism in favor of such heterocosmic quests as impressionism and surrealism. Litterateurs have been slower to ease up, but that is only to be expected, given that they took much longer to develop convincing techniques of realism. Nowadays, most literary creativity is heterocosmic to some degree, and only those writers and critics stubbornly enmired in nineteenth-century mud still insist that dogged naturalism has any natural entitlement to be considered virtuous.

Throughout this evolution, however, one thing does stand out even to the most cursory survey: the vast majority of heterocosmic works of art do not, in fact, make the slightest attempt to represent better worlds than the one that we experience. Instead, they deliberately set out to depict worlds that are even worse—which might, if appearances are not deceptive, have been made by Gods even more imbecilic and much crazier than the divine prat who might, were we not wise enough to realize, or optimistic enough to hope, that such chaos cannot have been planned or intended, still be credited with designing ours. Nor is this merely a matter of statistical majority; the few artists who do set out to represent worlds that are nicer and more peaceful than ours do not get any credit for their noble intentions, let alone their achievements. Hardly anyone wants to read Utopian or Arcadian fantasies about worlds in which all the characters are eternally happy and nothing ever goes awry. Even in the fields of popular fiction where "happy endings" are compulsory, those endings are most satisfactory when they are hard-won, against the odds stacked by an essentially hostile and sadistically menacing milieu.

It is almost as if the primary function of art, so far as its producers and consumers (if not its philosophical observers) are concerned, were to examine exactly those phenomena which make the experienced world seem less than perfect, often exaggerating them as well as bringing them into urgent focus. If so, it would not be in the least surprising. Given that no one with an atom of common sense or imagination could possibly believe that the world could not be better than it is, the business of everyday life is bound to be a problematic matter of coping with its defects. At the very least, literary endeavor might be able to help us by reassuring us that those difficulties, even at their most vexatious, can be successfully met and overcome—that is the essence of a "happy ending"—and more ambitious literary labor might actually be able to do more than that, by providing clearer analyses of the form and dynamics of the world's faults.

Although this kind of work can certainly be done in a naturalistic context, investigating the ways in which such faults are routinely expressed in the actual world's everyday transactions, there is also something to be said for the kind of experimental isolation that creates imaginary settings in which those faults may be given greater liberty to run riot. There is even a case to be made for the construction of "exotica"—imaginary worlds so unlike our own as to be almost incredible, in which the everyday transactions of the actual world are rudely shoved aside, and the goalposts of possibility awkwardly shifted.

There is a philosophy of imaginative fiction—often summarized by reference to a dictum suggested by H. G. Wells—which suggests that heterocosmic innovations are best used sparingly, strictly rationed to one per plot. That method certainly fits in with elementary experimental design, as developed and sanctified by the scientific method, which aims to isolate single variables in order that their particular concomitants can be identified. It has, however, recently been pointed out that if any of the six fundamental constants of physics were varied even slightly, the universe would not be capable of containing life—a discovery that supports the biological observation that small mutations are usually deleterious. It is only by varying more than one—and perhaps by modifying all six—simultaneously that a hypothetical physicist can create an opportunity to find other viable combinations. In much the same way, it is only by throwing away an entire organic scheme and designing a new one from first principles that natural selection can build viable new orders, families and species.

It is, similarly, in the realms of gaudy exotica, rather than those of minimal distortion, that adventurous artists might hope to find something genuinely new, interesting and exciting. Most of the time, of course, they will only succeed in concoct a dog's breakfast—but that's life, in a world that is blatantly not the best possible, nor even a conspicuously laudable effort. There's no harm in trying, and no virtue in refusing to try, so I do.

"Beyond the Colors of Darkness", "Enlightenment", "A Saint's Progress", "Black Nectar" and "*Danse Macabre*" are original to this volume. "Nephthys" first appeared in *Peeping Tom* 13 (1994) and was reprinted in a Necronomicon Press chapbook, *Fables and Fantasies* (1996). An earlier version of "An Offer of Oblivion" first appeared in the October 1974 issue of *Amazing Stories*. The first version of "The Dragons Alziluth and Yetzirah" appeared, as "How the Dragons Alziluth and Yetzirah Lost the Knowledge of a Million Lifetimes", in *Star Roots* 1 (1989); the present revised version first appeared in *Fables and Fantasies*. "*Mens Sana in Corpore Sano*" first appeared in *Violent Spectres* 2 (1995). "Plastic Man" first appeared in Swedish translation in the *Norcon 99 Program Book*; this is its first appearance in English. "Aphrodite and the Ring" first appeared in *Scheherazade* 11 (1995) and was reprinted in *Fables and Fantasies*.

BEYOND THE COLORS OF DARKNESS

When the news reached the city of Is that the Lady Valeria had died on the isle of Ouessant, to which she had been taken in triumph by her latest princely lover, the entire city gave itself over to an orgy of mourning. When a great lady dies far from home, all resentments are forgotten; all of those who had been numbered among her admirers—whether they were men or women, old or young—were ostentatious in their weeping, while all those who had hated or despised her pretended otherwise.

Is was not to be drowned for a hundred years and more, and no Christian missionaries had yet arrived from the East to tell its innocent populace that its nobility was vile and decadent. Its aristocrats were magnificent in their conscienceless, and Lady Valeria had been the most magnificent of them all. She had also been fortunate enough to leave the city before her beauty had begun to spoil, leaving a rich legacy of envy behind.

Although the golden wine of dreams and its dark companion had already become exceedingly rare within the walls of the city, many a glass was raised to the Lady Valeria's memory, and its contents avidly drained. Many a luxuriant and lustful dream was born of those sorrow-stricken draughts, but the flames that burned in her former lovers' hearts could not be extinguished so easily. Those who knew real grief yearned for more potent cures, while those in whom the flame of desire was too bright to be quenched affected to yearn for a darkness deeper than any connoisseur of the Underworld's dark wines had ever contrived to discover.

It is said that time heals, and it is undoubtedly true that the majority of men is so poorly equipped by treacherous memory that their pain soon disappears beneath numbing scars. On the other hand, there are souls so very sensitive that time seems to them to bring naught but further torment: men in whom the bloody wounds of honest memory seem to gape ever more widely, shedding their vital fluids with unabated profusion. These are the rare beings who believe that they might die of love or grief, and for whom the combination of the two seems to be a living hell that cannot long endure. It chanced that there was a young man among the Lady Valeria's most recent lovers—the last-but-one in a sequence said to extend into the thousands—who aspired to be of this dire kind. His name was Multipliandre.

Had he spent longer than a few months in the ranks of the Lady Valeria's discarded conquests Lord Multipliandre's face and health might well have been despoiled by jealousy, and he would certainly have been divested of his newly-inherited fortune by the various species of carrion crows that prey on the lovesick and bereft. As destiny dictated, however, the news of her death found him still young, strong and handsome—and richer by far than any young, strong and handsome man ought to be in a city as civilized and decadent as Is. He promptly fell ill, as propriety demanded, but it was widely suspected among his friends, servants and neighbors that his determination to die was not as strong as he affected, and that he would soon rediscover the utility of forgetfulness.

When Vulgric the Vendor of Exotica slipped into the alleyways of the Low City from the quay on the western side of the great Sea Gate, the rumors he heard in the taverns soon brought him to Multipliandre's wrought-iron gate, anxious to exploit an opportunity that might not long endure. Lord Multipliandre had instructed his servants that common hawkers were not to be tolerated even at the tradesman's entrance, let alone the main gate. Had the lord's instructions been dutifully followed, such a visitor as Vulgric would not only have been refused entry but given a severe beating before he was sent on his way, but the Vendor of Exotica was, as his unorthodox trade demanded, an unusually persuasive man. Within minutes of presenting himself at the gate Vulgric was ushered into the bedroom where the unfortunate Multipliandre lay, pretending to slink by slow and agonizing degrees towards one of the more ignominious of Death's many doors.

"I desire nothing," Multipliandre told the Vendor of Exotica, meaning—probably without consciousness of the underlying hypocrisy of his declaration—that what he desired to the exclusion of everything else was oblivion.

"Then you are in luck, sire," Vulgric said, "for nothing is exactly what I have to sell—and I pride myself on offering a quality of service in that regard which no one in the world can match."

"You are ridiculous," Multipliandre told his as-yet-unwelcome visitor. "Every marketplace in the civilized world is full of greedy merchants who have nothing to sell, and every one of them is determined to get the highest possible price for it. You are also a fool. Had you been sufficiently discreet to remain on the public side of my threshold I could only have had you beaten for knocking at my gate, but because you have crossed it I can do with you as I like. I shall have my servants flay the soles of your feet, in order to offer a stern lesson to anyone else who would dare to trespass on the tolerance of a man who is dying of hopeless love."

"The soles of my feet have been flayed before, my lord," Vulgric told him, negligently, "but the skin eventually grows again, if one is prepared to be patient. Somehow, I doubt that your own servants have had practice enough to perform such an operation with the skill requisite to render the pain unbearable. In any case, I have not come to despoil the heart-rending tragedy of your ostentatious mortality but to make the experience of suffering more interesting and worthwhile than you might be able to contrive without expert assistance. I have come to offer you the distilled essence of the flower that men call Black Nepenthe, which grows where no star has ever shone—not even the baleful stars that ordinary sight cannot perceive."

"Madman," said Multipliandre, "I have drunk the golden wine of dreams and tasted every single one of its rivals, including its most lugubrious kin. There is no narcotic in the world more powerful than the blackest of the Wines of the Underworld, which is the very essence of velvet darkness."

"I am the sanest man alive," Vulgric assured him, "and no trader who has ever lived has had a keener ear for a bargain than mine. I despise those greedy merchants who have inferior varieties of nothing to sell, and are determined to sell them as dearly as possible, for they are liars and cheats to a man. I alone have the Black Nepenthe to sell, and I never ask more for a price than its exact and authentic worth."

"No alien intoxicant is dearer to connoisseurs of oblivion than the beloved Black Wine of Is," Multipliandre told him—but it was obvious by now that he was intrigued, and might be glad to be convinced that he was wrong. No matter what perverse delight a man may take in the insistence that he is dying of love-inspired grief, he is always willing to be told that there is something in the world capable of easing his torment, especially if he is wise enough not to be entirely honest in his determination.

"The darkness that is known and celebrated in Is merely consists of the absence of the five ordinary colors," the Vendor of Exotica told the bed-ridden lord, "whose number coincides with the number of the ordinary senses and the number of fingers on an ordinary hand. But you will see, if you care to look, that my hands are by no means ordinary."

As he spoke, the Vendor of Exotica raised both his hands, with the palms open, so that Multipliandre could see that each of them had seven fingers, counting the thumb. What was even more intriguing was that each hand had an eye in the middle of the palm.

Multipliandre had not spent half his meager life in the company of magicians and half his brief love-life in the arms of a sorceress without hearing rumors of the kind of eye that can be concealed in a man's fist, and the extraordinary powers of sight that such eyes often have—but he knew enough to be wary of imitations, so he said: "In all the cities bordering the great forest of Lyonesse, and all the islands in the vast Sea of Yroise, men see seven colors in the rainbow."

"That is not true," Vulgric said, contradicting him in a casual manner that warranted far worse tortures than flayed feet. "They try with all their might to see seven, because they know in their hearts that there ought to be seven, but it is fatuous to pretend that orange and indigo are distinct colors. There are five ordinary colors, and those are the colors that ordinary men see. Those are the colors whose superabundant sum is the gold of sunlight and the wine of dreams, and those are the colors whose subtraction leaves as its remainder the darkness of the so-called Black Wine of Is and other ill-reputed Wines of the Underworld. Extraordinary men, on the other hand, can see seven colors when they raise their hands towards the firmament, and various mixtures of two when they look into what other men call darkness. They alone are equipped to seek out the deepest absence of all: the void from which even the hidden colors are banished; the emptiness beyond the color of darkness; the oblivion of Black Nepenthe."

"Will it help me?" demanded Multipliandre. The grief-stricken lord believed that he only desired to know whether Black Nepenthe would guide him to one of Death's less ignominious doors, but he was deceiving himself in that belief. Perhaps he did not deserve an honest answer—but it is a paradox of human intelligence that men besotted with self-deception and arrogant pretence are always in direr need of honest answers than those endowed with clear sight.

"Why else would I be here?" asked Vulgric, disingenuously. "Am I not the most honest tradesman that there ever was?" He, at least, was never guilty of self-deception, although there never was a trader incapable of arrogant pretence.

"And the price you will doubtless ask," Multipliandre said, "is everything I possess—given that I am generally considered to be richer than I ought to be."

"Everything," the Vendor of Exotica observed, "is certainly the roundest sum of all, which saves the bother of arithmetical haggling—but I am a reasonable man, modest in my needs. I would not dream of trying to agree a price until you have tasted a drop of my produce, so that you might be sure of what you are buying."

Multipliandre had been on the point of demanding a sample of the hawker's wares, and had been fully prepared to insist, but the trader's apparent generosity made him suspicious. He told himself, however, that a man in his tortured state of mind should have no refuge left in his heart or soul for cunning or subtlety. "It is the least I could expect," he said.

"You may taste two drops, one by one," his visitor told him. "The third, should you desire a third, will have to be purchased, at the price I name." As he spoke, he closed his unnaturally crowded hands and lowered them to his cummerbund of black silk, whose folds were twisted in a most peculiar fashion, as if they were cracks in the fabric of reality. He brought forth therefrom a silver-coated crystal phial, whose mirrored surface distorted the image of the curtains that hung by Lord Multipliandre's bed, so that they seemed to stretch like the languid forelegs of a yawning cat.

It cost Lord Multipliandre a considerable effort to raise himself from his pillows. His wounds were in his memory and his affections rather than his flesh, but he considered that the torment of a sensitive soul ought to be reckoned all the purer for that, and no less debilitating. He had to lean forward and tilt his head backwards, so that Vulgric could place a supportive hand behind his blond head.

The trader tipped the phial with minute exactitude, so that a single drop fell from its mouth on to his avid tongue. Although it hardly seemed possible that a drop so small could dissolve the whole body of a man like Multipliandre—who was slim, but tall and very adequately muscled—it could and it did. The young lord felt his entire being turn to liquid as he entered into the droplet and became quite lost in its colorless depths.

He understood immediately that those depths were, indeed, quite colorless. They were blacker by far than any darkness he had ever known before. While he was thus immersed he became an extraordinary man, who could see perfectly clearly that there was another black beyond the ordinary black, a void from which the two politely unobtrusive colors of common-or-garden darkness had been conclusively banished. He could also see, with equal clarity, that Death's doors were more numerous than he had previously suspected.

In the heart of the droplet there seemed to be a solid tomb, hewn from a mineral darker by far than jet or obsidian. Multipliandre judged that it must contain the finest sepulcher in all the world, where time would stand so still that millennia might creep past in a moment, utterly unheeded by patient dreamers of the eternal dream.

It seemed that the door of the tomb opened to receive him, and that he flowed into it, in the guise of an unexpectedly liquid phantom. It seemed that the lid of the sepulcher was raised to welcome him, and he poured himself into its loving mouth, which savored him voluptuously, as if he were a draught of vintage wine, a harbinger of inspiration and intoxication. In due course, he was swallowed and digested; the slow flux of his consumption and transfiguration was a blissful corrosion, an ecstatic surrender to eternity.

It was a wonderful dying, so far removed from the fevers of the flesh that such petty ideas as undying love and unbearable grief were rendered quite devoid of meaning. This was a graceful and aesthetically purified dying: a dying truly fit for a young and excessively wealthy lord, if such a fortunate individual could ever be convinced, in his heart of hearts, of the necessity of rushing to Death's embrace.

Hell, Multipliandre realized, was a crude artifact of imaginations nourished by the five ordinary senses and the five ordinary colors. Beyond the colors of that kind of darkness, which was still palely lit in the sight of the kinds of eyes that nestled in exotic palms, there was a velvet darkness made for men of exceptional sensitivity. That darkness was absolute, and it was eternal, and there was nothing Hellish in it at all. It was a truly aristocratic darkness, far above the morality of common men and far beyond their fear of pain.

Then the sepulcher raised its lid, and the tomb opened its door again, and spat him out. The droplet evaporated, so abruptly that Multipliandre was precipitated out of it in an exceedingly undignified and discomfiting fashion. He found himself back in his flesh, back in his bed and back in his narrow room, in a worse condition than before. He no longer felt the exquisite pain of his lost love, but he certainly did not feel better than before.

Mirrored in the silver body of the phial the young lord could see his face peeping through the sinuously moving curtains of his bed. He could see that his hair was no longer blond but white: the purest kind of white there was, compounded out of the five ordinary colors and the two mysterious others, cleverly mixed to avoid the golden excess of sunlight, fine wine and glorious wealth.

Multipliandre looked at the back of his hand then, and saw that its joints had become gnarled, its skin wrinkled, and its hairs as long and as pale as fragile ghosts. When he turned the hand over, the eye that looked back at him from the palm of his hand was bloodshot and terrified. It stared at him as if it were the eye of a madman who no longer wished for sanity, but only for release.

"Will you take the second drop?" asked Vulgric the Vendor of Exotica. It was a rhetorical question; the merchant knew full well that he had made his sale, even though he had not yet quoted his price.

The second drop did not dissolve Multipliandre as the first had done. His body had become so utterly desiccated that his tongue had the texture of dry bone, and it sucked up the tiny tear of darkness in a trice. But the tear was salt, and served only to increase his thirst, and the once-young lord felt the dryness spreading through him, turning flesh and bone alike to alabaster, and then to dust.

For a fleeting moment, the cloud that Multipliandre had become was white, but the whiteness began to fade from it as soon as it began to drift on an insistent breeze, which quickly became a gale. By the time the color of Multipliandre the Cloud had turned to an ordinary black he was a thunderhead in a great storm: a warrior in the wild hunt of the night. He realized then that the great majority of Death's multitudinous doors were far from quiet, and the great majority of Death's lustful caresses far from tender.

When the once-young lord became truly black, having passed beyond the binary colors of darkness, he began to discover joys that he had never known in life: the corrosive rapture of wrath; the scathing exultation of slaughter; the fabulous rage of battle. There had been great warriors among his ancestors—how else could the fortune he had recently inherited have come into being?—but he himself had been a civilized man, protected by the walls and sea-gates of a great maritime city, and the temptations of knighthood had never punctured the envelope of luxury that had surrounded him since infancy.

Now, he had lightning at his beck and call, and the roar of thunder to express delight in the power of his bolts. He howled with glee as only a storm cloud can, and the fire of his fury rained down upon the fertile Earth, his ferocious lightning burning and desiccating everything and everyone it happened to touch.

Peace, Multipliandre realized, was an artifact of an intellect nourished by the five ordinary senses and the five ordinary colors.

Beyond the colors of the kind of darkness that was still languidly lit in the sight of the kinds of eyes that stared out of exotic palms, there was an avid, famished darkness made for men of exceptional appetite. That kind of darkness was insatiable, and it was infinite.

Then the cloud turned to rain and hail, and cast Multipliandre down upon the sodden ground, where he was spread-eagled in an exceedingly painful and undignified fashion. He found himself back in his flesh, back in his bed and back in his narrow world, in a far worse condition than before. He no longer felt any pride in himself—neither in his wealth, nor his beauty, nor his capacity for the finest feelings of which humankind is capable, nor even in his capacity for the exercise of power and destruction—and he felt far worse, in consequence, that he had ever imagined that it might be possible to feel.

Mirrored in the silver body of the phial the ancient lord could see his face, far withdrawn behind the shuddering curtains of his bed. He could see that his cheeks and forehead were as white as a blanched skeleton, and that his bloodless lips had drawn back from his strangely-elongated and curiously-pointed teeth. The only vivid color left in him now was the color in the irises surrounding the black pupils of his eyes, which were as red as blood.

Multipliandre looked at his hand again, and saw that his fingers were now seven in number, each one of them a talon tipped with a horrid claw. He saw that the eye in the centre of his palm had become insolent, and that it was staring at him with a contempt so naked as to be unendurable.

He realized, belatedly, that he had not really wanted to die in response to the news of the Lady Valeria's demise, and that it would have been wiser by far to greet the news casually, or even with a sarcastic laugh. He had been a fool—but he realized, too, that the city of Is had been so very full of fools that his foolishness had faded into a background which had only seemed colorful to blissfully uneducated eyes.

He was no longer a fool, but that was not to his advantage—unless, of course, he could define his desires to suit his new intelligence.

"The third drop of Black Nepenthe," Vulgric the Vendor of Exotica reminded him, "will seal the bargain. You know, now, what the price must be, and how meager your notions of everything and nothing used to be. You know, too, that there was no deception in my claim to be a reasonable man, modest in my needs."

Vulgric made not the slightest pretence of asking a question or pausing to await an answer; his speech merely served to confirm an arrangement already made by placing his seal upon it—except that the seal was not his, and nor was the bargain. He was merely a Vendor of Exotica, working on behalf of the Dwellers in Ultimate Darkness, who were utterly and rightly scornful of petty Hells.

As the third drop of Black Nepenthe met Multipliandre's thirst, he felt himself transformed by a process of divine metamorphosis into a fabulous insect: a jeweled and sacred scarab, as black as the black beyond the colors of darkness, but glossy nevertheless, with a sheen uncorrupted by the slightest hint of gold. He shone with a mercurial reflected light that no ordinary eye would have been able to see or comprehend.

The sacred scarab compounded out of Lord Multipliandre and the drop of Black Nepenthe flew through the infinite and eternal night of nights, over a million tombs and oceans, through a million storms and battles. In the beginning, it flew beneath the baleful light of a trillion stars invisible to ordinary eyes, but as it flew the stars grew further apart, expanding into the ultimate void, and their light was lost in distances unimaginable to the inhabitants of the narrow city of Is and he globe on which it formed an infinitesimal speck.

Eventually, Multipliandre the Insect came to the borderlands of the imagination and the intellect, where no sun or moon had ever shone, nor any star, however baleful.

There the flower grew from which the Dwellers in Ultimate Darkness, which Vulgric the Vendor of Exotica served so faithfully, distilled the most precious of their earthbound wares. It was a vast bloom, more beautiful by far than any flower ever beheld by the eyes of common men, although its color was the purest black of all. It was beautifully unilluminated by any paradoxical light, but Multipliandre had evolved beyond the necessities of the vulgar sense of sight. He knew that he had never been in touch with reality, until now, nor even with his own true self.

He was wise, now. He was no longer capable of taking pride or pleasure in that acquisition, but wisdom was its own reward. He knew, and understood, that he had never wanted to die. He also knew, and understood, that it was too late to quibble about such irrelevancies as death.

The bell of the flower was filled with plangent sound, both soothing and sublime. As Multipliandre the Infinitesimal flew into that lovely cacophony, every fiber of his evaporating being vibrated boldly, each in sympathy with its own particular resonance.

He could not see that the pistil of the flower was shaped like a mailed hand grasping a mace, but he knew it. He could not see that its anthers were tipped with the heads of lovely women, each with the tresses of that same fabulous blackness devoid of the colors of darkness, or that their lips were engorged with blood, but he could imagine it.

Multipliandre the Absent did not know that while he tumbled into the depths of the avid flower, shedding the remnants of his wings as he went, that the edges of the petals making up the rim of the bell had closed behind him, sealing him in. Nor could he imagine the black cylinder shrinking around him, although he did know when it closed about his lovely body that he was no longer dreaming of flight.

He did not fear that he would be digested, for he knew by now that Death had more doors than he had previously been able to imagine, and that the most grandiose were not necessarily the most sought-after.

The flower's demanding embrace reminded him, in a curious but not altogether unkind fashion, of the urgent embrace of Lady Valeria. Her lovemaking had always had something of the dark about it—but he had never realized before what those dark caresses lacked, in addition to the five colors of ordinary light.

He understood that now. His fate was neither to be dissolution nor dissipation, but to enter into Chaos, there to become an Element of Confusion.

Had he been in any condition to think or dream, Multipliandre the Nonexistent might or might not have taken some faint and febrile comfort from the knowledge that of all the merchants in the world who might have sold him nothing at a grossly inflated price, he had been fortunate enough to meet the most honest.

Meanwhile, Lord Vulgric the Master of Exotica arose from his bed with delighted alacrity and put on his best suit of clothes. He summoned all his servants, and told them that it was high time they received proper and adequate training in the art of flaying. Then he went in search of the inheritor of Lady Valeria's reputation as the most beautiful woman in Is, who—although she probably did not realize it, as yet—was in dire need of the skilled and cunning courtship that only a man who was younger and richer than he ought to be could possibly provide.

He knew that his life was destined to be short, and he intended to make the most of it, calculating the measures of his self-indulgence with skill and sense.

AN OFFER OF OBLIVION

Of all the adventures that a man may choose to undertake during a lifetime spent in a universe without maps, the loneliest and most futile is surely the Starman's Quest—the search for the perfect world. The wanderer must go on and on, from star to star, with no chart to guide him, unable ever to return home. In order to become a Questor he has to abandon his origins—cut them right out of his soul. A Questor has no birth, no past, no race, nor even, properly speaking, a species. His only alternative to the terminal Quest is to be claimed—adopted and consumed by alien ways. There are worlds that can make such demands on a man that they simply swallow him up—take him away from the stars and digest him—but they cannot give him back his birth, his past, his race or, properly speaking, his species. They can only make him an offer of oblivion.

Simeon and Lazaro Ferrara were remarkable because they started the Quest *together*. The Starman's Quest is essentially a one-man affair, but Simeon and Lazaro were brothers who had lived so closely together throughout their lives that they considered themselves to be more one man than two. They were twins, but they were by no means identical. They were sons of different eggs, and some had been known to suggest that they must surely be sons of different fathers. They had never questioned their mother about the matter. It was not important; they were bound together all the more closely by their dissimilarities.

Simeon was short and slim and dark, and very fierce. His intensity of manner and the power of his will were very pronounced. Nobody is born a Starman, but it seemed that if there ever were a child who would be forced by circumstance to reach out and grasp the stars, then it was Simeon Ferrara. Lazaro, on the other hand, was massive and ruddy and very strong. He was full of force but it was all buried somewhere inside his bulk, and the only one who knew how to unlock it was Simeon.

The planet-hugging people of their homeworld always used to say that Lazaro was the real man and that Simeon was his shadow. In the star-worlds, where humans thought differently and not-quite-human people more differently still, they laughed and said that Lazaro was an empty fat man and that Simeon was the thin man who should have been inside him. Lazaro and Simeon were more inclined to class themselves as the immovable object and the irresistible force, in that order, but it was a mere affectation—a private joke. None of these descriptions, of course, was in any way adequate to identify the very special bond that existed between them, but their glibness and their simplicity can offer some hint as to the depth and richness of that bond.

They lifted from their homeworld during their nineteenth local year, when they were even younger in standard terms. They competed for the honor of being the first to forget its name as they followed their unplotted course through the universe without maps. Their first spaceship was a glorified skiff named the *Smiling Sphinx*. It leaked air, and everything else. They were lucky to survive their first few trips, but they usually were lucky. The Cosmic Whim appeared to have a considerable prejudice in favor of brotherly love during that standard year.

The last of their seven spaceships was called the *Nightingale*. That was the ship in which they began the Starman's Quest. The ship in which you begin the Starman's Quest is invariably your last ship, because your ship is an integral part of the Quest, your silent partner. If the ship goes down, so do you. Lazaro and Simeon were seventeen years older than the day they had gone out to the stars when they acquired the *Nightingale*. Seven ships in seventeen years hints at a good deal of prosperity, and they had, in fact, been favored by the currents of trade. They were never single-minded and occasionally serendipitous. Starlife never does run smoothly, but Lazaro and Simeon achieved a comfortable metastability. Lazaro's strength and Simeon's drive were equal to almost all situations. All in all, they were a good combination, and both true servants of the stars. (There may be sons of the soil, but there are only *servants* of the stars; that is one of the many corollaries of the Cosmic Perspective.)

At thirty-six years of age, Lazaro had a receding hairline, and the florid quality of his complexion had been exaggerated by the caresses of a thousand suns. His immense strength was undiminished, and his excess weight had not caused him to become lethargic. Simeon, however, looked five or six years younger than his brother. He was still wiry and dark, and as full of fire as ever, but with an added artistry of thought and movement—an augmentation which suggested, undeceptively, that the years had been generous to him while they had only been kind to Lazaro. The brothers had not quarreled in a very long time; they had put childhood behind them when they lifted the *Smiling Sphinx*. Their closeness had fulfilled them both.

The brothers accepted the Starman's Quest with the absolute assurance that a perfect world for the one could not help but be a perfect world for the other. They were undoubtedly right. Had they ever been numbered among those few fortunate individuals who are rumored to have found perfection, then it would surely have been a shared perfection. It is impossible to imagine it any other way. This story is, however, no mere wistful rumor. They did not succeed.

The meaning that the Quest held for Simeon and Lazaro Ferrara was exactly the same as that for other men—which is to say that it was a kind of damnation. The years marched by, and the knowledge grew in both of them that they were never going to succeed in finding the perfect world. They lived, as we all do, on hope, but hope is inevitably subject to the steady and unrelenting assault of failure. They found ten worlds that were no use to them, then a hundred, then a thousand. There were always a million more scattered throughout the sky, but a human being is only a human and a human life is only a pitiful measure. Failure adds up. Disappointments and discouragements accumulate, little by little, into a terrible load. A Questor can never stop his load from growing, let alone lighten his burden. He cannot settle for anything less than success. In time, even the seconds that pass by in transit seem to add measurably to that load. Hope remains—it is unvanquishable—but it reclines in a bed of weariness and lassitude. Eventually, it even ceases to hurt, but acts as an anesthetic instead. At this point the Starman's Quest manifests its hollow, uncompromising choice, which is, empirically speaking, the last and final choice: multiply failure until the load kills you, or accept another offer of oblivion.

Only when they came to this, the last of all choices, did the differences between Simeon and Lazaro prove more decisive than the bond combining them. They were, after all, two elements and not one. Fifty years had never contrived to pull them apart, but the Starman's Quest finally imposed its stern logic upon their unnatural union.

On a world called Berenita, they were offered a choice that only one of them could make. It happened to be Lazaro. He had only to say no, as he had done countless times before, but every single one of those denials had been an honest answer to an honest choice. This time he said yes, and that was an honest answer too.

The woman's name was Myrca.

It had to be a woman, of course—but it was not quite as simple as that. Simeon and Lazaro were way beyond youth and romance. Their love for one another was easily competent to conquer any claim that might be made on their love from outside. It was not love that Myrca offered; it was oblivion. She offered it to Lazaro. Simeon would have refused out of hand. He had the ultimate intensity of determination. He was the irresistible force. There was nothing in the Universe that could have turned him aside from the Quest once he had embarked on it. Lazaro did not have the same intensity of purpose. It was not that he found the burden of failure to be intolerable, but simply that he could not face its rate of inexorable increase forever. *His* load was an immovable object, and he knew that it would kill him soon. He knew that Simeon would outlive him by some years, and that his brother would have to be alone someday. He accepted that, but Simeon could not.

The Cosmic Whim, of course, was empowered and entitled to send them both to their deaths at one and the same instant, or to separate their dying by exactly the few seconds that had separated their being born, but that is not the habit of the Cosmic Whim. It might favor brotherly love, when the mood takes it, but it is always an implacable enemy of linear symmetry. If, as some philosophers suggest, it is merely a mirror to the human mind, a myth invented in the image of its maker, it is a distorting mirror. How else could it be honest?

Myrca's body was ivory white. Her scales were silver and pearly. Her eyes were wine-red. She was not beautiful. She was an empath—not a vulnerable empath, but a radiant empath—and she was a singleton.

Radiant empaths are not particularly rare; nor are vulnerable empaths, although they always go crazy and usually die young. Singletons, on the other hand, are rare. Myrca was one of the rarest of the rare breed. Most radiants shine only with love, and who needs a radiant empath to bathe in love? Even the sourest, sickest man can generate love within himself if he really needs it. But Myrca radiated something that most humans cannot synthesize, in spite of its existential value. She radiated—and hence appeared to *be*—*ataraxia*: calm of mind, or, to put it more accurately, stillness of soul. Myrca was heart's ease. She was more than mere contentment; she was peace itself. Very few men find peace. Many people do not even know how valuable it is, but Questors always do, because it is intrinsic in the nature of the Quest.

Lazaro Ferrara found Myrca, and for Lazaro she shone; for Lazaro, she *wanted* to shine. It hardly seems fair that such a gift should be so fragile that it should be for one man and one only, but Myrca was one woman and one only, and there *is* such a thing as balance in the Universe, no matter what cynics might assert. Even if Simeon *could* have shared that peace, he was not offered the choice, and could not have agreed to any such arrangement. No man has a common soul with another, no matter how close their material selves might be.

Simeon Ferrara had to lift the *Nightingale* from Berenita alone.

Before doing that, Simeon argued with his brother. When he saw that argument could not prevail, he *begged* his brother to come with him. He pleaded. He tried to weep, but he could no longer contrive tears. Lazaro had always wept most of the tears they had wept between them, and that had eventually come to seem sufficient. Lazaro did weep, but it made no difference.

"Somewhere, my brother," said Simeon, when he accepted that the immovable object had triumph, however unreasonably, over the irresistible force, and that he had to go on alone, "there is a planetary paradise. Logic insists that it must be so, for the mapless universe is exceedingly large and it contains innumerable Gaean clone-worlds, on which the laws of spontaneous generation have inevitably produced analogues of human life, whose variations mimic the variations between human individuals. I shall find that paradise. I *must* find it now, because you've made it impossible, or at least inappropriate, for me to die without finding it. I *will* find that planetary paradise, Lazaro, and when I do, I'll bring the news back to you, because paradise is the only thing that can take you away from here, now that you've given in to the sloth that always threatened to claim you, against which it was my mission in life to fight."

"The planetary paradise is out there somewhere, my brother," agreed Lazaro, "but it's far outnumbered by overt and covert versions of Hell, and that makes Hell a good deal easier to find. You and I have come too close to Hell on many occasions, and I've always thought it likely that you might get a good deal closer yet, if you aren't careful. Perhaps it was my mission in life to prevent that from happening, but if so, I give up. I've chosen peace instead of the overt and covert dangers of Hell, and I don't think you should blame me for it. I assure you that you can't tempt me away from peace with the lure of paradise, because *my* Quest is finished now. My starlife is over. Go find the planetary paradise, Simeon, but please refrain from bringing me any further news of the stars, because it will only hurt you if you do. I wish you good luck."

"I will go," said Simeon, "because I have to—but I also have to come back, and I don't think that you should blame me for it. I need you, Lazaro, and it really doesn't matter to me that you no longer believe that you need me. This is one world that I'll always be able to find, even in a universe without maps, and I can't be content simply to leave you here."

"I'll always be glad to see you," Lazaro said, "but it won't make any difference."

All these words tasted bitter when they were spoken, and left an aftertaste that was distinctly unpleasant, but each of the brothers knew that the other did not wish him any harm. There was no malice at all between them. Each of them did what he had to do, and if the impulses that drove them generated into a kind of war between them, it was a war that they could not help but fight, and they fought it lovingly.

Lazaro stood on top of a lonely hill, surrounded by the scents of a multicolored summer, and watched the *Nightingale* rise into the sky on a plume of fire, taking his brother back into the wilderness of stars. He knew that Simeon had told the truth when he said Berenita was the one world that he would always be able to find again, even though neither brother, by now, would even have known where to start looking for their homeworld. In the midst of his infinite peace, however, Lazaro realized that he had never quite managed to forget the name of the world that had once been his home, and he wondered whether Simeon had won that particular competition.

Five local years—the equivalent of seven standard years—had passed when Lazaro heard the engine-song of the *Nightingale* again, as she sank through another summer night to land upon that same hill. The meeting between Simeon and his brother was a joyful one. The joy stirred Lazaro's peace and brought him echoes of pleasure and adventure, and it lightened Simeon's dark despair for a few nostalgic moments. While Myrca sulked because Lazaro was diverted from her, Simeon gave an account of the worlds that he had visited and what he had found there. Time had buried the bitter resentment that he had felt at the time of the parting, and Simeon felt almost sure that the lure of the stars would draw Lazaro away from his peaceful half-existence.

Simeon told Lazaro about his setting the *Nightingale* down in the drylands of Della Strada, where he had been able to earn a good living hunting jeweled snakes in order to buy fuel to lift the ship again. He had been forced to work twice as hard as he had become accustomed to do, because he was working alone for the first time, but he had avoided the snakebite that might have condemned him to stay there forever while the snake-healers doled out their antidote on a daily basis in return for his labor in the dessert.

Simeon told Lazaro about Capua, Bakhout, and Kilifi, and the acute trading of subtle biotechnologies between the three worlds that had turned him a steady profit on the money that was left over from Della Strada. On Molvedo, though, he had been forced to go back to work as a gem-miner in a rare conglomerate of tertiary matter, which had been recycled twice over by supernoval blasts—a freakish statistical abnormality, given the relative youth of the universe, even taking into consideration the notorious lumpiness of galactic matter and the vagaries of dark matter distribution.

In the gem-mines Simeon had met and worked with Cormac Alcala, who had achieved some small celebrity among the starworlds of the Arm as the Starman Who Could Not See Stars. A strange vengeance had been taken upon Alcala by a rich groundhugger to whom he owed money; he had been subjected to intimate psychosurgery, in order that he could no longer see the starlight that lit his Quest. The trick had not, of course, put an end to the Quest; nothing could do that. Simeon and Alcala had worked together on Molvedo and had proved moderately successful, but they had gone their separate ways thereafter.

Then Simeon related incidents that had taken place on Ramiflora, Veronique, Cap Estel and Tirynthe. Lazaro listened to all of these anecdotes, and he was moved by the stories. He could imagine the brilliant blueness of Ramiflora's sun, the shelled aquamen of Veronique, the steel supercities of Cap Estel, the relics of the War of the Kilkon Empire on Tirynthe. The stars whispered to him, with Simeon's voice, and he was tempted. The allure of the million worlds, with their limitless offer of experience, was something that he could not entirely ignore—but he had already chosen to accept the ataraxia that Myrca radiated, and there was no going back on the choice. He told Simeon that he was contented and secure, and that he would stay on Berenita.

Simeon realized then what he had known all along, but had not yet admitted to himself: that his brother was not to be wooed back to the starpaths by mere traveler's tales. Time was not on his side. Lazaro's ataraxia was unshakeable by nostalgia. Simeon concluded, as logic forced him to do, that if Lazaro were to be won back to the Starman's Quest, then it would have to be done by the power of a tremendous bribe, or by naked force.

Simeon returned to the Quest after a matter of days. Myrca was glad to see him go. Lazaro was not—or, at least, could not admit to himself that he was.

This time, Simeon went to the ruined world of Chebec and the mechanized superstate of Volokon. He visited the death-worshippers of Yami and the light-masters of Olein. He fought deadly space-storms to reach the distorted surfaces of Firdaussi and Lycaon, and the so-called mirror-world of Taj Dewan. This time, however, he was not simply following the same kind of capricious course that he had followed previously with Lazaro. This time he was *searching* as well as Questing—searching for something that he could use to buy his brother back from the radiant enchantress.

Simeon did not know exactly what he was looking for, but he never allowed himself to doubt that he would find it. He believed, with all his heart, that there had to be prices higher than the price of ataraxia—which was, after all, mere passive peace. Simeon knew that, in a Universe that might not actually be infinite but might as well be, from the human point of view, there was a price appropriate to every possible purchase. He did not bother to calculate the probability of his finding the appropriate price, and he refused to consider the possibility that he might not know it if he found it.

As time went by, among the stars, Simeon told himself, insistently, that time *might* still be on his side. Myrca was only a woman, and she was growing older. Could her radiance resist the ravages of aging? Could it possibly be so attractive, even if it were sustained, when her beauty began to fade? In the form and tenor of this argument, however, Simeon's gathering desperation was clearly evident even to him. He *needed* to believe that he could win Lazaro back. He could not bring himself to believe anything else.

The ghostfolk of Chebec's Lands of Blackened Ruin offered to teach him arcane mystical techniques that allegedly empowered the mind to manipulate dark matter and dark time to material advantage, but Simeon knew that he could not fight Lazaro's peace with vulgar magic tricks. He understood that ataraxia and mysticism are similarly counter-dynamic and anticipated that his brother would think the latter only a shadow of the former.

The masked priests of Yami were known to possess a drug that could make humanoids of any age and species seem younger and more handsome. They would not release it except to the most committed followers of their nihilistic faith, but there were many Questors prepared to fake that sort of sincerity in the interests of prolonging and facilitating their searches. Unfortunately, no drug is without side-effects and psychotropic side-effects routinely impose heavy costs; although it really did blunt the effects of age, the Yamian potion also sharpened the fear of death. Simeon would have procured some, by any means necessary, if he had been able to convince himself that it might have the effect he required of it, but he knew that a potential extension of life would be several undermined by a loss of confidence in its possibilities—and he knew, in any case, that Lazaro was unlikely to trade his hard-won maturity for the glamour of a new youth while he was at peace with himself.

Simeon found an alternative technology of emortality on Olein, but the potential cost to the recipient was, again, considerably higher than the far-from-exorbitant price that the light-masters asked for it. He might have bought immortality for his brother and himself merely by disposing of the few meager gems that Cormac Alcala had smuggled out of Molvedo, which Simeon had then stolen from the Man Who Could Not See Stars, but it was not the sort of emortality that could be enjoyed in a human body on a Gaean clone—they would have to become alien sun-dwellers. Simeon was well aware that mind and body could not be dealt with quite as casually as the light-masters suggested. To accept what the light-masters offered would have been to surrender humanity—and that, almost by definition, amounted to one of the many versions of Hell that were so much easier to find than paradise in a not-quite-infinite universe.

On Firdaussi, and again on Taj Dewan, and yet again on Casorati, Simeon found opportunities to become immoderately rich for the first time, but those were cloud-nebula worlds, and the opportunities involved the risks of time-chasms and space-lesions. He weighed the chances very carefully, because he wanted to be able to pay the price of what he needed to find, if and when he found it, and he knew that it probably would not be as cheap as Oleinic emortality, but in the end he decided that the star-worlds had better offers to make to a man of his particular talents and inclinations.

On Lycaon, the indigenes assured him that they could sell him better dreams than any available on any other word in the galaxy, let alone the Arm, but they were not convincing. On Noemi it was glory of which the natives claimed to have the best supply, but they were obvious charlatans. On Athdara, the planethuggers boasted that they alone possessed the panacea, and they were certainly healthier than any other race that Simeon had yet encountered, but he knew full well that a little dis-ease is not a dangerous thing, and that Lazaro already had his fill of ease.

On Hadad, a boundless, storm-torn gas-giant, the silver-haloed cryptomorphic hive-people offered Questors a silk-textured dust unusually rich in imprisoned dark matter—which, they claimed, made it uniquely subject to metamorphic transmutation into anything the humanoid heart might desire. They offered to throw in the secret of manufacturing authentic ecstasy for free, as an added inducement. Hadad's hive-dwellers also claimed, quite plausibly, that theirs was the richest world in the galaxy. They intended to become a great deal richer yet, by the simple stratagem of investing all their profits in new enterprises, their own personal needs being very simple.

Simeon eventually contrived to persuade himself that he had found what he needed on Hadad: not mere happiness, nor ultimate love, nor vulgar power, nor even the secret of manufacturing authentic ecstasy, but the darkly-endowed dust that was the necessary raw material of any conceivable metamorphosis. He began to assemble the fortune that he needed to pay the price for a handful of that dust, carefully and cold-bloodedly. His stolen gems could not provide him with the wealth that he needed, and most of the tasks he had previously undertaken to earn his fuel would not have returned such rewards in an entire lifetime.

He became an assassin on Heres, quit while he was still unrecognized, and bought himself into a worldshaping business in the Nightscar cluster. He refitted the *Nightingale* as an exotic particle trawler with a fifty-parsec net, and drove it through the hazardous hyperspace of a nascent nebula called the Cloak of Blood; from the bleeding suns within it he took enough strange matter to manufacture a twist of crystalline time, and forged a molten wu-matrix to contain it. With the proceeds of that sale he bought the planet Paradine, and used it as collateral for further loans. Four days later he bought Angelet, then mounted a relentless commercial assault on the shareholders in a vast but undercapitalized star-trawling combine. Within a week he controlled the entire fleet, and his subcontractors stripped the Cloak of Blood, the Catacrypt and the Scorpio Pit for half a standard year. They took sixty per cent casualties in the process, but the ensuing shooting war was a mere formality—the rebels eventually surrendered on all seven of the worlds where they had attempted to withhold their hard-won goods, and Simeon stripped all seven worlds of their wealth by way of compensation. Then he took the whole of his fortune to Spiridion.

Simeon's intention was to lay a single bet, hoping to double his fortune at a stroke. There were plenty of other gambling worlds in the Arm, but Spiridion was the only one where whole worlds were routinely staked and no wager of any magnitude was ever refused. Simeon knew that if he were to win, that doubling would take the mass of his capital over the critical threshold, beyond which it could be made to increase constantly without any effort at all, at a rate of growth that was acceptable to the Hive of Hadad.

Simeon knew that the wheels of Spiridion were a trifle crooked, but he also knew that the Cosmic Whim is capable of defeating any house percentage, if it happens to be in the mood, and he was riding such a colossal victory tide at that particular moment that he was convinced that Spiridion's entire Aristocracy of Chance would not be able to match him, in any game they cared to choose.

He played the Unlimited Wheel, and he won.

Simeon claimed his handful of silky-fine dust from the Hive of Hadad, and preserved it carefully. He did not intend to keep a single grain for himself. It was all for Lazaro. He carried it back to Berenita, still flying the *Nightingale*, although he would have been able to buy any ship in the Arm on the day he left Spiridion, without affecting his ability to pay the price of the dust.

He told his brother the whole story—every detail of his adventures and every element of his reasoning. He was, by that time, absolutely certain that Lazaro would understand everything this time, that Lazaro would appreciate all the terrible risks he had taken, that Lazaro would be awed by the unparalleled magnificence of his success, and that Lazaro would accept the proffered gift gladly, and would return to the Quest.

Lazaro refused.

Simeon's winning streak was over. It had lost out to radiant ataraxia, to the feeble glow of peace of mind.

"I have no need of any metamorphic potential, external or internal, my brother," Lazaro told Simeon. Then he took his brother to see Myrca. Myrca smiled. She was no longer afraid of Simeon Ferrara.

Simeon saw that Myrca had grown older, but that she had grown older with a certain strange majesty. She had never been truly beautiful, but now she had a carriage and a style that made her former self seem pale by comparison. Myrca had benefited from her love-affair with the Starman, just as Lazaro had benefited from his love-affair with the empath. Lazaro still loved her, and was still at peace with life, death and the Universe, even though he had never found paradise. His was a relative contentment, but it was enough. He had no wish to return to the Quest, at any price.

Simeon was stricken by confusion and desperately sad. He clung hard to his futile belief that Myrca would eventually begin to lose her battle against the ravages of age, and that when she did, her hold on his brother as bound to weaken—but Lazaro and he were now old, by any standards, and Myrca had a good few standard years in hand of them. For the first time, Simeon felt the closeness of death, and he knew that there was only one thing left that he could realistically try.

He also knew that Lazaro knew—but Lazaro was at peace with himself and the world, and could not resist. If Simeon simply cared to render his brother unconscious for a few hours, he would be able to take him far enough away from Berenita in the refitted *Nightingale* to make certain that they would never be able to find their way back in a universe without to maps. On the other hand, if Simeon wanted to do so, he could simply kill Myrca and destroy Lazaro's peace, giving his brother no alternative but to board the *Nightingale* of his own accord.

Simeon wanted to do either or both of these things. He believed that the Starman's Quest was far more important than any man's peace, but the strength of his own need only served to remind him of the strength of his brother's. Simeon loved Lazaro, and he found it difficult to override that love and draw his gun.

The stars in the maples universe have the answers to all problems, though, and this was a very easy answer for them to provide. Where you can buy peace and dreams, youth and ecstasy, emortality and the power of metamorphosis, you can also buy misery and remorse, despair and pain, callousness and covert kinds of Hell.

Lovelessness comes cheap.

When the *Nightingale* lifted from Berenita for the third time, Simeon was in search of something quite different from his earlier objectives. He was no longer at pains to avoid the many kinds of Hell with which the universe is scattered; he wanted to buy one. He wanted to buy the freedom to forget his brother's need and fulfill his own. The difference between them, unapparent for fifty years, had finally driven them to all-out war.

Simeon was an old man by now, and he was giving way to obsession. A younger Simeon might have been unable to do what the old man now chose to do, but the older Simeon's loneliness had become a curse, and rendered his life and his identity meaningless. In all probability, his love would have been doomed by circumstance alone, and he would not have had to make any purchase at all had he had more patience. As things were, he merely sought to confirm the fact by paying a price.

It was on Salamandra that he bought what he needed. It cost less than a thousandth part of what he got in exchange for the silken dust, even though he was prepared to sell that for a fraction of its real value. The trip took more years out of his life, though, because in reaching Salamandra he passed through Lalika and La Carelle, Isfabva and Ferriol, Hypericum and Cinna, and half a hundred other worlds whose names he did not take the trouble to remember. He took his time. He was fighting himself, because it was that kind of war. In any case, he knew that although release might be cheap and relatively easy to obtain, he sought a particular kind of release that many men needed but few were willing to buy. In the end, though, the *Nightingale* alighted yet again on the fire-swept hill, and Simeon went to meet Lazaro with a crash-gun in his hand.

The Cosmic Whim has never been an admirer of violence as a means to the romantic end. It had long ago lost its sympathy with Simeon and Lazaro Ferrara and their Starman's Quest. It had already cheated and defeated them both.

Lazaro was already dead, and his peace was now eternal. He had not waited to feel the pain of meeting his brother for one more time. He had died still cherishing his love for Simeon and the assurance that Simeon loved him. Myrca was there. She was full of love, but she could not radiate ataraxia any longer, for anyone. The threat of time was clear in her less-than-beautiful features. Simeon wept tears of frustration and defeat when he saw his brother's grave.

With Lazaro's death, Simeon found that the Quest was over for him too. It had no meaning for him now that he was truly alone. Beside his brother's grave he prayed for another offer of oblivion; he prayed for a peace of his own. He asked Myrca to love him as she had loved Lazaro. She told him that she might have loved him once, but that he could never have loved her. She could not give him peace, even if she were still a radiant empath, because he had already given away his heart.

Perhaps she was only being cruel in telling him that—punishing him for the fact that he had come to her with a crash-gun still in his hand. It is difficult to believe that Myrca could have ever loved Simeon, and more than he could ever have loved her.

He was tempted to kill her, but he did not do it. Instead, he lifted the *Nightingale* from the hill that shadowed his brother's grave and flew her back to Spiridion, which he had no difficulty in locating eve in a universe without maps. There he took his fortune back to the Unlimited Wheel.

This time, he was not playing to win.

ENLIGHTENMENT

The forests of Christendom were vast before Rome fell, and they remained vast for a thousand years thereafter, until progress finally cut them down to a manageable size. The heart of each such forest remained more distant from human civilization than measurements in miles can possibly suggest, often containing woods and groves whose roots extended deep into the Underworld. It was in one such wood that Huon of Bordeaux, traveling much closer to home than the reassuring versions of his legend suggest, once met Oberon, the king of the Underworld, and joined in a contest of wits with that monarch.

In sweetened and Christianized versions of legends borrowed from the Old Religion, Oberon is represented as the King of Faerie—which, after a fashion, he was and still is—but one of the soothing functions of legend in Christendom has always been to prettify Faerie in all its sinister aspects, and make it seem harmless. After Huon's reputed success in wining Oberon's amity, many other errant knights sought solace, shelter and kindly magic in the wilder parts of the eternal forest, but most found only pain and desolation. If there had ever been such a strange thing in the mortal world as an honest storyteller, humans might be less susceptible to such delusions.

Most of the people who live on the fringes of the forest are honest worshippers of the Christian God, and many of those who live closer to its heart still follow the more caring traditions of the Old Religion, but there are parts of the forest, even today, that are host to the worshippers of darker gods, including the gods of the Underworld. One such region is to be found in the lower reaches of the mountains that extend in an arc from the port of Is in Leonais to the western edge of the plain in which the city of Rennes now stands. The Underworld is, of course, worldwide, and everywhere as dark, except in those regions to which Oberon imports his own treacherous light, but his worshippers in that lonely region believe that the chthonic king has a particular fondness for some of its grottoes.

The uncomforting legends of the Old Religion, which are by no means as soothing as those of Christendom, allege that the grottoes in question were once briefly donated by Oberon to a company of demonic glassworkers, who worked by his royal decree to produce a number of magical windows that would let a more colorful light into the Underworld by magical means. All but a few of those windows were eventually integrated into the walls of Oberon's many palaces, but some were rejected for that purpose because the workmanship was not as perfect as he desired. Some of those rejects were stolen by unruly servants of the great king, and sold for petty silver on the surface, to human devotees of the dark gods—but none endured for long in the building in which it was placed, for they were all smashed by the crusading knights of Bretagne, who knew danger when they saw it.

The broken windows were carefully buried, and the knights who had disposed of them believed them lost forever—but time passes far more swiftly in the sun's realm than it does in the obscurity of Faerie, and things change there at a hectic pace. Even great cities are sometimes lost in the sea, huge hills worn down by wind and water, and new edifices raised on the cryptic foundations of ancient ruins. In the mortal world, lost things have a habit of reappearing—or, at least, of sending forth faint echoes into the fragile souls of human beings.

* * * * * * *

On one of the lesser crags of the Monts de Bretagne, near a town called Kervesal, there once stood a fortified house, which was a centre of forbidden worship until a king who was but distantly related to the luckless Anne who married Charles VIII of France appointed his champion, Lanval de Karys, to lead a crusade against such relics of Druidism.

All good Bretons have heard fanciful tales of that great adventure, although no one now knows more than a tiny fraction of its facts and events, and legend still takes leave to celebrate Lanval's victory over the magic of the evil enchanter Andrealphus Alio—but the versions of the tale that you might have heard from other tellers undoubtedly ended with the moment of Lanval's victory, and with the implication that all has been well in Kervesal's neighboring estates since it was achieved. Alas, it is a truth which we too often forget that the shadows of evil cast by black magic often linger long after the destruction of the black magicians themselves.

It was because he knew this that Lanval de Karys, having acquired the estates of Andrealphus Alio by right of lawful conquest, caused the enchanter's fortress to be razed to the ground and its stones scattered about the mountainsides by his men-at-arms. Lanval never set foot among the ruins again, and when the time came for him to die—which he did in his bed, as all great heroes deserve to do, though precious few achieve it—he advised his son Guillaume to let them well alone. Guillaume, being a wise man as well as a dutiful son, did as he was instructed.

Guillaume lived ten years less than his father, departing this life at the age of fifty-two, and was unfortunate enough to die far from home, while fighting a campaign for his liege-lord the king. In consequence of this, his own son and heir, Jehan de Karys, acquired the lands around Kervesal without receiving any solemn warning in regard to his use of them. All his knowledge of them, in fact, was drawn from the enduring tales of his grandfather's glorious victory, which the local story-tellers had altered considerably, for the purposes of flattery.

Jehan loved to bask in the reflected glory of his ancestor's heroic exploits, to the extent that he took an early opportunity to visit the ruined mansion of Kervesal, and was somewhat surprised to discover that the people of the town were not particularly grateful for the privilege of receiving him. He was a young man still, and had not quite understood how happy common men can be when their liege-lords live distantly, and do not put them to the trouble of providing obligatory hospitality.

When Jehan proudly rode up the slope to Andrealphus Alio's blasted fortress, in order to inspect the scene of his grandfather's victory, he was unlucky enough to be thrown from his horse. He fell awkwardly, splitting his head upon a square-edged stone. Although his skull was not cracked, the wound never fully healed, and for the remainder of his life Jehan was tormented by evil dreams and periodic bouts of madness, during which the ordinary light of day seemed to him to be eclipsed by a brighter and more colorful light, whose constant changes made him dizzy with dire anxiety.

Jehan became convinced that the ruins of Andrealphus Alio's citadel had a curse upon them—although whether he was mad or sane at the moment when he was persuaded of it, none can tell. For this reason, he inserted a clause into his will which specified that the hill on which the fallen fortress stood should be set aside from the demesnes of Kervesal, and should not be handed down to his own eldest son, who was called Lanfranc. Instead, the hill was given to the Sisters of Saint Syncletica, who had established a thriving abbey in Is, and whose order was expanding its numbers rapidly in consequence of the notorious decadence and rapacity of that city's merchant-princes, which greatly offended its pious citizens.

The clause also made provision for a company of master stonemasons and carpenters to be hired-from as far afield as Paris, if necessary—to assist the sisters in building a house of God on the site, the sanctity of which was bound to defeat and dispel and further lingering effects of the enchanter' curse. By means of this device, Jehan de Karys sought to erase the last vestiges of the legacy of Andrealphus Alio, whose prayers had been offered to a deity very different from the Christian God.

* * * * * * *

Catherine, the Mother Superior of the Sisters of Saint Syncletica in Is, was not entirely delighted to receive news of Jehan de Karys' legacy following his death. It was not that she feared any curse that might lie upon the land, but simply that the region was remote, and reputed to be a lair of heretics whose customs and practices posed an even greater danger to the moral welfare of her younger charges than the lascivious merchants of the city. She felt compelled, however, to accept the gift of the land and the services of the artisans.

Jehan's son and principal heir, Lanfranc de Karys, was also less than wholly delighted by the fact that the Sisters were to inherit land that might have been his, but it was such useless land that he reconciled himself to the loss without overmuch heartache. He declined, however, to meet the costs of the artisans' raw materials—which his father had forgotten to mention in his will—in addition to their living expenses, which had been stipulated. He sent them instructions to use the stones of the demolished castle to build the nunnery that was to be raised in its stead. Although the greater part of the rubble had been tipped into the moat surrounding the house, and could not be taken out again without a great deal of excavation, the stonemasons agreed to do this if he would pay the wages of a handful of local laborers to do the digging. To this, Lanfranc consented, albeit with an ill grace

In consequence of these decisions and negotiations, a small company of the Sisters of Saint Syncletica was dispatched from the house in Is along with the artisans who would build their house, in order to cook, clean and mend for the workmen and make preparations for the eventual accommodation of a larger population. The nine Sisters who were appointed to this mission accepted their lot meekly, as they were bound by their vows to do. Some, indeed, were quite pleased by the prospect. For Sister Theresa, who was given authority over the company, it was a welcome opportunity to train for an eventual promotion to the rank of superior; and for the likes of Sister Petronilla and Sister Morwenna—neither of whom had ever taken to city life—there was the lure of the green forest and the fresh mountain air. There were also some whose uncomplaining acceptance masked a certain quiet unease, however, and one of these was Sister Agatha.

Agatha was twenty-two years old, and had served Saint Syncletica for eight years. She was the daughter of a craftsman glassworker in the service of one of the merchant princes of Is, and she had been placed in the care of the Sisters purely and simply because her father had feared—probably quite rightly—that she was likely to be debauched by his employer almost as soon as she attained puberty. Her aptitude for holiness had, alas, failed to mature in parallel with her body, and she found the life of a nun exceedingly tedious. Mother Catherine had attached her to the company in order that she might be kept busy, and thus protected from the substitutes for work that the Devil sometimes make for idle hands.

The hardship of the early days spent on the slopes above Kervesal kept the nine Sisters very busy indeed, for they had to undertake such tasks as ferrying water from a rather distant well—in far greater abundance than was required for cooking and washing—and clearing land for a vegetable garden in order to facilitate the initial labor. The back-breaking nature of this work left them exceedingly weary by dusk, and could not help but magnify any resentments that the Sisters might have felt against the burden of their discipline. It was summer, but the nocturnal weather was often chilly and damp, and although the builders immediately set out to erect two temporary wooden barracks—one for themselves and one for the Sisters—their progress on that project, as well as the larger one, was painfully slow to start with. The tall trees that had to be felled for timber to make the barracks had heartwood that was uncommonly hard and resistant, which blunted the carpenters' drills and saws, and the huge black stones that had formed the walls of Andrealphus Alio's citadel were exceedingly difficult to raise from the former moat, even with block-and-tackle.

For the first two weeks, the whole company shivered in tents. After that, however, things became gradually easier. A pump was set in place to bring water to an artificial basin close to the site; the soil in the vegetable-garden was turned over, weeded and planted; and the barracks were completed. The work the Sisters had to undertake became less burdensome, and the free time that they had each day to spend as they pleased was subject to a significant increase.

Although she was far from being the tallest or the strongest of the Sisters, Agatha was freed from cooking and cleaning duties in order that she might help the workmen in their lighter tasks, fetching and carrying for individual artisans, bracing planks or mixing mortar. The work was sufficiently hard that her back still ached and her hands often became blistered, but it often looked far harder to uninformed observers than it really was. Sister Theresa, thinking that Agatha was in sore distress because of the blisters on her hands, lightened the burden of her duties even further, telling her gently that sunlight, fresh air and proper rest would soon bring more color to her pale cheeks and more strength to her slender limbs. Grateful for this consideration, Agatha sometimes exaggerated her own tiredness, and was glad that her natural pallor resisted the burnishing effects of the sun.

The Sisters and the workmen moved into the two wooden houses as soon as the roofs were in place, although they were by no means quite finished. Each of the sisters was allotted a room that was bare-floored and bare-walled, but not unduly uncomfortable, being an exact copy of the rooms in which the artisans slept. Agatha thought it better than the stone cell she had occupied in Is—but her relief did not last long. While the masons and carpenters remained in their barrack-room, Sister Theresa decided that the cellars of the old house—which had now been cleared of accumulated rubble—would be very easily adaptable into proper cells, with the aid of a little cunning improvisation.

This improvisation took some while, but Agatha could easily have wished that it had taken a good deal longer. Before the end of summer, each of the nine Sisters was accommodated in a stone cell again, with a pallet on which to sleep and two candle-brackets for light. Eight of the cells were grouped into two sets of four, but Agatha was given one that was somewhat apart from the rest and had the rare privilege of a small unglazed window looking out over the sheerest slope of the crag—an indulgence, because Theresa felt that Agatha was still too pale and needed extra light.

So black was the stone of which the walls of her cell were made, though, so narrow was the window, and so poor the quality of candles manufactured in Kervesal, that the Agatha's cell seemed dreadfully gloomy to her at first—so gloomy that she even risked broaching the subject of a return to the wooden hut, which fell on deaf ears. As time passed, however, she grew to like it better.

Although Agatha's cell, like all the others, was in the cellars of the old house, its position above a sheer drop made it possible to imagine that it was actually set high in a tower, and she took what comfort she could from this pretence. It faced west, so the sun only shone directly through the narrow window when it was setting, but she was not displeased by that; she liked the roseate tints that the clouds took on which there was a margin between their extent and the horizon. The window overlooked a stand of uncommonly twisted trees whose tattered crowns, far below the window, seemed to mutter arcane imprecations when stirred by the wind, and that too she grew to appreciate, often pretending that the trees were whispering to her, like friends sharing confidences. Her fellow Sisters, alas, had very few confidences to share.

Sister Theresa instructed the Sisters to make their rooms fit places for prayer, first by staining the dark walls white and then by placing crucifixes on the walls. She also gave them permission to supplement the crucifix with images of the Sacred Heart and the Madonna, and to improvise images of other symbols associated with Saint Syncletica: a white dove in flight, and a veil spattered with tear-shaped drops of blood. All the Sisters found considerable difficulty in executing the first of these tasks, for the black stones that had once protected Andrealphus Alio were stubbornly resistant to the stain of purity, and whitewash had to be applied several times over before the walls would condescend to be lightened. Agatha found the task particularly frustrating, but in the end achieved a shade of grey which did not seem intolerably grimy.

By this time, the white habit that Agatha wore seemed to have lost its crisp cleanness forever, and no matter how she scrubbed it she could only bring it to the same shade of grey which she had contrived to impart to the walls of her room. Because she did not possess any icons or other paraphernalia of the faith, she took the trouble to make her own rather approximate design of a dove, but it did seemed a crude substitute for images of that sort manufactured in Is. She also outlined a white square on the wall, where the rays of the evening sun were able to strike it, which she dappled with droplets of blood from a cut on her hand, for want of any suitable pigment.

* * * * * * *

The people of Kervesal were not ungrateful for the Sisters' presence, for they had heard that the devoted followers of Saint Syncletica knew methods of curing the sick and easing pain. Mother Theresa received a steady steam of pleas for aid, which never went unanswered, and sometimes achieved an unexpectedly good result. Although no price was asked for such assistance, those villagers who were fortunate in this respect began to send gifts of food and livestock; by this means the Sisters acquired a flock of chickens and a milking-goat. The Sisters who went out to administer their medicines and nurse the sick also became inheritors of a rich tradition of cautionary tales and rumors that had been handed down through the generations from the times when Andrealphus Alio had been their oppressor.

Among these stories there were the usual horrific accounts of cannibalism and child-sacrifice that inevitably accumulate about repute enchanters, and the usual flights of fancy regarding storm-riding witches and demonic night-monsters, but there were other items too, more unusual and idiosyncratic, some of which were contained in popular sayings and cautionary rhymes, the import of which was no longer properly understood. One apparently-pointless tale alleged that Andrealphus Alio had made alliance with subjects of the king of the Underworld, from whom he had bought certain mysterious artifacts and from whom he had learned the art of staining glass. A mysterious proverbial instruction associated with this tale, which was known to every child in Kervesal—though none knew what it meant—bade anyone who dared to walk upon the nearby mountain slopes to *Beware the Glorious Light that floods the hidden valleys of the soul.*

Agatha took more interest in this eccentric tale than the more familiar ones, mainly because her father had been a glassmaker and she had always been fascinated by the fragments of puddled glass that he had sometimes given her as playthings when she was very small, deeming them too convoluted to make good windows. She had never quite understand why the citizens of Is wanted transparent windows rather than ones that were merely translucent, for she was usually frightened when she was taken abroad through the crowded streets, and preferred to draw a veil of distortion over such confusion. She liked looking through the bits of puddled glass, which confused what they did not entirely hide.

By virtue of the vows they had made, the Sisters of Saint Syncletica were not common women, but they still partook of the delight that all women find in fearful fancies and ominous whispers. They repeated the tales they heard in the local hearths to one another while they worked, and although they laughed as they did so—to demonstrate that they had no fear of the demons with which long-dead Andrealphus Alio had once made pacts—there was always a tiny thrill of anxiety in their laughter.

A great deal work still remained to be done on the house when the Sisters had whitened their walls and inscribed the sacred symbols of their faith. Although good progress had been made in excavating stones fro the former moat, the process of setting one atop another to form the frame of a new and more modest edifice had hardly begun. After long and careful consultation with the masons, Sister Theresa decided that the main body of the new nunnery ought to be erected on the site of the eastern tower of Andrealphus Alio's fortress, extending sideways to occupy the bulk of the former courtyard but leaving the outline of the original building's western face outside the nunnery's limit. This made good sense architecturally, but it had the odd effect of setting Agatha's cell—which was directly beneath the old western wall—outside the bounds of that main building. Sister Theresa did not think this important, and nor did Agatha. The old moat, which had been shaped like a horseshoe with an end-wall at either extremity, had not extended around that wall of the old house, because it was impossible of access anyway. The two end-walls of the moat had crumbled away to some degree, and that part of the ditch was rather unsafe, but there were no large stone blocks adjacent to the end-walls, which were protected by heaps of smaller debris, long overgrown by mosses, lichens and ferns. Similar heaps of fine rubble had trickled down between the larger blocks at various points along the curve of the moat.

Once the obscuring cloaks of vegetation had been stripped away, it quickly became clear that there might be a few useful things to be gleaned from this trivial wreckage. The people of Kervesal had doubtless made some effort over the years to search it for weapons and other items of commercial value, but they had not troubled to steal away such commonplace things as wooden bowls and clay goblets, or bronze cooking implements and copper sewing-needles, for which the thrifty Sisters of Saint Syncletica could easily find a use. Sister Theresa therefore appointed Agatha and Sister Columba to the task of sifting through the minor debris as it was gradually exposed and cleared, and to recover and repair anything which could be put to use.

This was a duty which Sister Agatha found at first to be even more to her taste than fetching and carrying for the masons and carpenters. It was far less wearying, and the pleasurable possibility that a new discovery might at any time be made was ample compensation for the dullness of most of the work involved. The work had its less pleasant side, for the artifacts buried in the rubble were sometimes to be found in association with grisly reminders of the fierce conflict that had raged around the fortress when Lanval had besieged and stormed it, but Agatha was not afraid of skulls and skeletons and parchment-like fragments of skin.

It was not Agatha who discovered the first pieces of colored glass; they were shown to her by a laborer who thought them odd, but too badly fragmented to be of any use or value—but the glass-worker's daughter knew how rare and precious genuine stained glass was, as opposed to glass that was merely overpainted, and she realized immediately that the fragments must have come from a window of extraordinarily good quality. She asked the workman to be taken to the place where the shards had been found, where she began to rummage about for others. When she found several more shards, some as large as fingernails and a few the size of copper farthings, she ordered the laborer to set aside his spade and proceed more carefully—which she was entitled to do, because he was a local man and not one of the imported craftsman. She asked him to collect all the pieces of glass he could find, and any strips of lead which might once have been used to bind them together. In the meantime, she hurried off to tell Sister Theresa what she had found.

Sister Theresa was less enthusiastic than Agatha expected. Al though she was city-bred and had seen painted glass windows in the houses of noblemen, Sister Theresa had never looked at the windows of the princes of Is with the proud and interested eyes of a glassworker's loving daughter. In fact, she considered all such decorations to be mere frippery.

"I suppose you had better collect all you can," said the Superior-in-waiting, dismissively, "if you think it might be of use or value to someone. Perhaps, if you can assemble enough to reformulate a picture of some sort, we might make a gift of it to Lanfranc de Karys, in order to appease him for the loss of his land and the cost of our artisans. He seems to be the kind of man who might take pleasure in toys and baubles. I dare say that he has a clever window-maker at his beck and call, if you cannot make anything of the fragments yourself."

Agatha was annoyed that her discovery should be so casually minimized—and, as it seemed to her, that her father's calling should be so casually dismissed. However, she took what had been said to her as permission to make an effort to recover as much of the window as she might, and to do with the fragments whatever she could. She therefore gave Columba and the workmen instructions to be very careful in working near the spot where the first fragments had been unearthed, and to save all the shards which they found, no matter how tiny. For the rest of that day and all of the next she waited fretfully nearby, ready to pounce on any glint of colored light that might show as the rubble was scraped away from the rock that lay beneath.

By the evening of the second day Agatha had hundreds of pieces of glass in her possession, and dozens of pieces of the lead that had once outlined the pattern of the window. The idea was born in her mind that if she could recover a sufficient number of fragments she might eventually be able to reconstruct that pattern—enough of it, at least, to guess what had been depicted there. She had no delusions as to the difficulty of the project, but she felt compelled to make the effort, so she cleared a space on the floor of her room and began to lay out the pieces there, shuffling them around in the hope that she might begin to see some semblance of order amid the chaos.

After an hour's pondering—which somehow used up the time which she should have spent at her private prayers—Agatha was forced to admit to herself that the task seemed hopeless. Although she had collected a good many fragments, many of them quite large, it was obvious that they were only a small fraction of the number into which the window had been shattered. She guessed that the vast majority of the remaining fragments must be very tiny, and would be very difficult to recombine even if they could eventually be found. Because she had no idea what the pattern had looked like, it was hard to know where to start in trying to rebuild it.

More fragments of colored glass turned up on the next day, and a few more on the next, but the workmen had completed the preparatory work of clearing the moat by then, and it was obvious that no more pieces would be thrown up by the appointed routines of labor. Agatha turned her attention to the heaps of earth that had been shifted from the platform that would form the foundations of the new nunnery, and to the sheer but cluttered slope that descended from the crag's western rim. She knew that much of the original rubble from the felling of the tower must simply have been tipped over that edge, and she suspected that a good deal of the glass from the window must have gone with it—but the slope was very steep, and the workmen had no intention of clearing the undergrowth from it.

Sister Theresa soon relieved Agatha and Columba of the task of sorting through the debris, on the grounds that everything useful had now been recovered, and gave Agatha—who still seemed to her to be too pale and frail for overmuch heavy work—a new list of domestic duties to be carried out in the cellars. Agatha had no option but to accept them, but found that they were sufficiently lenient to allow her a few hours of spare time, even during the hours of daylight. She began to use these hours in looking for more fragments of glass, wherever she thought they might be found—and she found enough, day by day, to make her feel that it was worth her while to persist in the task. Indeed, she came gradually to believe that she had a special instinct to guide her search, which might eventually bring it to a successful conclusion.

* * * * * * *

As the autumn gradually gave way to winter, the hours of daylight decreased markedly and those of darkness expanded in proportion. This steadily reduced the amount of time which Agatha could devote to her search for pieces of glass, but increased that which she could devote to her attempts to figure out how the pieces which she had might be connected with one another. This puzzle became very absorbing indeed—so much so that it routinely absorbed the time which should have been given to her devotions—but when Sister Theresa once suggested to her that she might be neglecting her prayers, she denied the charge vehemently.

There were several occasions when she was brought to the brink of despair, and became convinced that her project was hopeless, but on each occasion her half-formed resolution to give it up was subverted by a sudden gleam of inspiration that showed her how a group of pieces might be slotted together, or where a junction in the lead could be reconstructed and patiently sealed. Eight years as a Sister of Saint Syncletica had taught Agatha many things, including the value of patience, and an occasional happy discovery was enough to persuade her that the task should not be abandoned.

While the pieces remained scattered on the floor of her room she could never leave them alone for long, but was always drawn irresistibly back to the puzzle. Her moments of insight gradually accumulated into an emergent understanding of the form and organization of the original work of art. She discovered that the window had been circular, and that there had been several concentric circles within the outer one. She deduced that the blue and purple glass belonged mostly to the outer circles, with more vivid yellows and roseate shades closer to the centre. She realized that the innermost circle had contained a detailed image of some kind, perhaps a representation of a bird with golden plumage.

Each of these discoveries reinforced her resolution, and encouraged her to increase her efforts, which she began to do by denying herself sleep. It was soon noticed, however, that Agatha was burning more candles than any three of her companions, and she was summoned to the Superior-in-waiting to explain why this was so. She took Sister Theresa to see her work, quite certain that the sight of the partially-reconstructed window would be sufficient explanation and excuse, but the Superior-to-be had no notion of it as an intriguing puzzle to be solved, and could not see the picture emerging within the confused array of lead and glass. Sister Theresa saw the broken pattern as a silly and trivial mess, and said so.

"You must see, Sister Agatha," Sister Theresa said, in what was intended to be a gentle and kindly fashion, "that the objective cannot be worth the effort. What could you possibly gain by completing a task whose achievement would bring no worthwhile reward? You must understand that it is not fitting for a devout Sister of Saint Syncletica to become obsessed with worldly things. A window of colored glass, however beautiful, can only be a window on the mundane world. Our ultimate concern is to bring the mercy of Saint Syncletica to those who suffer grief, pain and desolation of the heart, not to play with ornaments."

Agatha accepted these rebukes very mildly, but her penitence was feigned, and she was very glad that Sister Theresa did not think to offer a specific instruction commanding her to abandon her work. Nevertheless, she did resolve to try harder to perform those observances which her faith required of her.

For some days she was unable to collect more than a handful of very tiny fragments of glass from the slopes beneath the burgeoning temple. Nor, in those few days, did she use more candles than any of the other sisters—but her enthusiasm for her task was not really lessened at all; almost every piece of glass which she found was now the cause of a tangible thrill, for she was very often seized by the conviction that she knew exactly where her new find would fit into the growing whole.

The outer circles of the window came steadily nearer to completion, and she soon redoubled her efforts once again in searching for the many fragments that were still missing. She spent a great deal of time clambering about the sheer slope beneath the window of her cell, or rooting in the undergrowth of the densely-packed trees, which now seemed more inclined than before to whisper confidences in her ears, and also to caress her with their skeletal branches.

When the outer circles of Agatha's window had been restored, save for a mere handful of fugitive shards, a most astonishing thing happened. There began to emerge from those outer rings of glass, during the hours of deepest darkness, an uncanny *glow*, which grew by degrees into a flickering blue radiance. It was as though the window was no longer laid out on a solid floor at all, but had been set in place to transmit the effulgence of a bright and exceedingly clear sky. Because the blues of the outer circle were mingled with purples and violets, the hypothetical sky often seemed a trifle crepuscular, and perhaps somewhat unearthly, but the glow seemed kinder by far than the dull yellow candlelight produced by local tallow.

Had Sister Agatha not been obsessively absorbed in her project, she might have been made anxious by this peculiar mystery. She might have remembered that this window had not been an ornament in some nobleman's petty palace, even in a city as corrupted by vice as Is, but that it had been a part of the fortified dwelling of the enchanter Andrealphus Alio, where it might conceivably have had some other purpose than mere decoration. She might even have recalled to mind the curious warning about "glorious light" that had passed through the company of nuns as an item of idle gossip and had attracted her particular attention at the time.

Had she been able to think in this way, Agatha would then have understood that her duty to Saint Syncletica demanded that she consult her Superior at once—but her mind was now preoccupied with other thoughts and desires, and she had already acquired the habit of secrecy. As things were, the thought that first sprang into her mind when she saw this radiance was that, in helping her to save candles, it would free her from further suspicion and pressure to abandon her self-appointed task.

Her stratagem worked well; Sister Theresa was satisfied with what appeared to be a return to a normal consumption of candles. By the same token, Sister Agatha was trapped in the unfolding web of her deceit, unable to seek any advice from her guardian with respect to the significance of the eerie light which lit her room for a few hours on either side of midnight. That did not seem to matter much, given Sister Theresa's earlier attitude to the window and the fact that she was not yet an authentic Mother Superior.

Agatha did not *feel* as if she was imprisoned by her deceit. Indeed, she felt more contented than she had ever been before. It was as if an eternal emptiness within her being, of which she had only been half-aware by virtue of its long familiarity, had been filled as neatly and softly as could be. She was now possessed of a sense of imminent completion, which all her sincere and heartfelt prayers to Saint Syncletica had somehow never contrived to provide for her.

Most of the pieces of glass to which her instinct now led her as she patrolled the slopes beneath the temple were roseate or golden in color, and the reconstruction of the circles to which they belonged soon progressed to the point where almost every piece could be put unhesitatingly into place. As these inner circles neared completion, they began to add their own measure to the light that poured into Sister Agatha's room in the winter dark, in such a patently magical fashion.

Agatha loved that light—which was certainly very beautiful—and delighted in studying its many changes. It was not in the least like true sunlight, for it had a ceaseless ebb and flow in it; what had earlier been a casual flickering was now a more tempestuous agitation. Whenever she knelt beside the window, bending over it in search of the place where a particularly problematic shard belonged, her many shadows would move on the whitened walls behind her like a troop of febrile dancers capering madly about a ritual bonfire.

The dingy walls of her room were quite transformed by the light of the window; their greyness was utterly banished by it, but the crucifix was cast into deep shadow. In the meantime, the sacred symbols of Saint Syncletica that she had improvised took on a new life, in which the ill-sketched dove became a deftly-drawn hawk and the blood-spattered veil came to seem much more vivid and personal. The perpetual dreary greyness of her habit was also redeemed, at least temporarily, for the strange and apparently sourceless light made it blaze with a new brightness, as if it were not a nun's worn robe at all but the brightly-colored costume of some courtesan in the merchants' palaces of Is.

Of the figure in the very centre of the picture, however, Agatha could as yet see almost nothing. There were only a few fugitive pieces of glass which seemed to belong there, which gave the merest impression of feathery form, without any proper indication of the configuration of the wings, nor the least sign of a beak or eyes. No light came, as yet, from the innermost circle of the window.

* * * * * * *

Agatha's quest was almost brought to an abrupt conclusion when Sister Petronilla and Sister Morwenna, who chanced one night to be returning from a mission of mercy at an unusual hour, reported seeing strange lights in her window from the path that wound its way around the foot of the crag. Agatha was summoned yet again to see the Superior-in-waiting. She became very anxious lest it be commanded that her work must cease, and she stoutly denied that anything unusual had occurred. She insisted that she had been asleep at the time the light was reported, and knew of no possible source from which it could have come.

Because Petronilla and Morwenna could offer no tentative explanation of their own, her word was accepted, but Sister Theresa did take the opportunity to question Agatha further about the fate of the stained glass that she had collected. Agatha denied that she was any longer interested in the reconstruction of the window, and said that, in any case, no sizeable pieces of glass had been found for some considerable time. Because the latter part of the statement was true, the whole was believed.

After this interview, Agatha took the precaution of hanging up a dark cloth to curtain the narrow window of her room while she worked, and whenever she went out she left the greater window on the floor covered by a mat that she had stolen from one of the carpenters.

That Sister Theresa believed Agatha's story was due in part to the conviction with which it was told, but also—as she gladly confessed to her ward—to the fact that Agatha seemed so healthy and cheerful nowadays that it was impossible for any of her fellows to believe that she was going without sleep. "When the Sisters first came to Kervesal, and for some time after," Sister Teresa told her, "you were so pinched in your features and pasty of face that I thought I might have to send you back to Is. You are not the strongest of the company, even now, but your skin has finally acquired a tan—a beautifully lustrous one, in fact—and your laughing eyes were as bright as a bird's."

Agatha was astonished to receive these compliments, for she possessed no mirror and had not had the least inkling of her own transformation, but she was glad to have them, and glad, too, that her companions were perfectly willing to attribute the change to the winter sunlight, the mountain air and honest labor—three things calculated to change anyone's complexion for the better.

Agatha no longer fell eagerly upon the few tiny slivers of glass that were occasionally found while work on the temple proceeded; indeed, she professed indifference to them. One way or another, though, the fragments eventually disappeared into her sleeves and pockets, and were carried anxiously at the end of each evening's communal prayers to the privacy of her room. There, the periphery of the innermost circle was slowly filled in, and she waited with rapt anticipation for the vital moment when the light that streamed through the outer circles would spread to the centre—when that enigmatic image would, as she thought of it, "catch fire".

She lived for that day; nothing else seemed to matter at all.

Unfortunately, the central motif remained irritatingly absent; there were a few fragments of glass that seemed to represent feathers, and enough lead to imply that the figure was the head of a bird, but of the beak and eyes there was still no trace. By now she had searched every inch of the slope beneath the burgeoning temple most assiduously, and she knew that there was little hope of finding anything but tiny fragments there.

Without the vital pieces, there was little more of the puzzle to be done, and nothing to occupy her hands and mind in those hours when the light of another world filled her room with its gorgeous colors. Her old habits reasserted themselves, but when she prayed—without taking care to specify which deity it was to whom she addressed her prayers—she prayed only for a further gift and a new revelation; her prayers expressed the yearning of her obsessive heart, which had no other object of affection than the face in the centre of the window.

When the winter solstice was passed and the days began to lengthen again, the strange light began to wax a little more brightly when it shone, and seemed more reluctant to wane thereafter. Every time it died away, Agatha went meekly to her bed, but on each following night, she was again so completely filled with the glory of the light that she was utterly entranced, and was very often driven out by the sheer fierceness of her hunger—not only out of her room but out of the house, whose dark wall now loomed up high above the crag, and only required a roof to become a worthy nunnery.

Winter was on the way out, but spring was slow to arrive and the nights were usually bitter. Snow often fell on the slopes, its whiteness all-but-invisible in the cloudy night—but there came a particular night when Agatha did not feel cold at all, and made her way unerringly to the whispering trees, which seemed to welcome her warmly even though they were bare of leaves and naked to the stars.

That night, someone was waiting for her in the shadowed grove. He carried no lantern and she could not see his face, but she knew by his short stature and his deep voice that he was not one of the region's villagers.

"I have something that you want," the stranger said, "and you have something that my master desires. Will you make a contract of exchange, so that your heart's desire might be answered?"

"I will," she said. She felt as if she were lost in a dream; in her dreams, she had never been prone to ask awkward questions, merely accepting things as they were, or seemed to be.

"Here is what you need," said the stranger. She felt a rough and hairy hand as he gave her a parcel of rags that had something wrapped within; she could feel hard surfaces and sharp-edges.

As the other turned to go, Agatha said: "You may take whatever I have to give, in return, as we agreed."

"It is already taken," he replied, although he had not asked her for anything specific, or accepted anything from her hands.

She took the parcel back to her room, and carefully hid it away before she went to sleep.

On the next night, when the half-completed nunnery had become quiet, Agatha uncovered the window to let free its turbulent light, and then took out her prize. She carefully unwrapped the bundle, exposing half a hundred pieces of colored glass and a few twisted slugs of lead.

The fragments of glass were mostly small and misshapen, and it was clear that it would be no easy task to fit them together in the correct order. It had been a long time since she had so many new shards to work with, though, and she was delighted by the challenge. Her nimble fingers began the work of turning and sorting, flying as if they were impelled by an intelligence other than her own. She felt as if she were laughing inside, but her lips made no sound; the silence would have been absolute had it not been for a sight wind rustling the branches beneath her window. She was very quick in slotting the pieces into place, for each one seemed to know exactly where it belonged.

The eyes she placed last, and when she placed them, she knew that her work was finished—that although a hundred tiny cracks and crannies remained in the grand design, she had done *enough*.

Incandescent light sprang from the heart of the window, and the figure detailed there was suddenly present in all its resplendent glory.

For a few fleeting seconds Agatha still thought that the figure was the head of a bird—perhaps the legendary firebird that built itself a nest once in every thousand years and then set fire to it, in order to be magically reborn from the flames. After that, she thought that it might be the head of a griffon, like the careful fake displayed as if it were a hunting-trophy in the palace of her father's master in Is. While its colors were still limned by curves of clotted lead it might have been either of those things—but as the cataract of light poured through the window between the worlds, the lead that held the pieces of colored glass seemed to melt and shrivel, so that the image ceased to be an image, and became reality.

Then she saw that the central figure was neither a firebird nor a griffon, nor any other mere animal intelligence. Plumed and crested with gorgeous feathers it might be, but this was a *person*, whose gaze was brighter with wisdom and knowledge than the eyes of any human being she had ever seen.

There was a tiny voice of warning within her, which tried to cry: "*Beware the Devil!*" in such a way as to make her afraid, but the voice seemed to Agatha to be no more than a tiny echo, feeble and forlorn—and if, as she freely supposed, it was the last vestige of that love and adoration which she had once given freely to Jesus and Saint Syncletica, its insignificance now was clear testimony of the transfer of her loyalty to another power.

The face that looked at her, out of that other world, which was so wondrously filled with ecstatic light, was incapable of smiling, for the black beak was set as hard as if it were carved from obsidian, and yet she was in no doubt that it was very glad to see her. She was perfectly certain that the creature whose head it was longed to enfold her in its feathery embrace, to cover her tenderly with the splendor of its fiery plumage, which was more golden than the setting sun, and rosier than the clouds that the sunset sometimes tinted.

The sheer beauty of the prospect overwhelmed her, and she threw her arms wide to welcome that transcendent embrace. Behind her, crowded upon the cold and narrow walls of that space that had been given to her for her allotted share of the world of mortal men, a hundred colored shadows strutted and jostled, as if utterly unaware of their own thinness and insubstantiality, uncomprehending of the fact that they were mere whimsies of a light from beyond the limits of the earth, playing in a darkness that was in fact near-absolute: the darkness of an Underworld, which could only ever be lit by the desire of King Oberon and the ingenuity of his subjects.

Agatha, who had once been a Sister of Saint Syncletica, gave voice to a liquid trill of pure pleasure—and those eyes, which she had so recently restored to their proper place, focused upon her an astonishing, appalling, avid look of love, full of laughter and the joy of life.

"There is light in darkness, you, see," said a voice as musical as the wind in reeds, echoing from invisible walls, "for those who can make their own windows, and seek their own enlightenment."

When Sister Agatha did not appear for morning prayers, Sister Columba and Sister Petronilla were sent to inquire whether she was ill.

They discovered her naked and supine upon the floor of her room, with her arms thrown wide and her legs apart.

It was, they said, as if she had been seared from top to toe by some incredible fire, which had burned her black. The walls of her room, and her discarded robe, were similarly black and ashen, except for a pair of crude designs that Agatha must have inscribed there herself: a strange bird, bearing some resemblance to a snowy owl, and a patch of white that might have be intended to represent a veil, stained with blood-red tears.

Embedded in Sister Agatha's seemingly-vitrified flesh, sparing not a single inch of it, were thousands upon thousands of tiny pieces of glass. It was almost as if her entire outer being had been turned into a bizarre window, which might or might not let in the light of the dewy sun to illuminate her soul.

Had they not known that it could not possibly be anyone else, Columba and Petronilla subsequently told their fellows, they could never have guessed that the strange object on the floor of the cell was Sister Agatha. She had been so utterly transfigured by her mysterious death that she might have been anyone at all.

THE DRAGONS YETZIRAH
AND ALZILUTH

The dragons Yetzirah and Alziluth were once the wisest beings in the universe, for they were heirs to a cultural heritage that extended over millions of draconian lifetimes—a period of time that amounted to billions of planetary years, because dragons are by no means short-lived creatures.

The preservation of this lore depended on there being two dragons, although each one was capable of reproducing without any assistance from another. As each dragon came towards the end of its allotted span it laid a single egg, which it subsequently swallowed. The egg was transmitted to an incubation chamber deep within the dragon's belly, and when it hatched the parent dragon would fall into a deep sleep while its clone-child consumed it from within, renewing the ancient flesh by reincorporation. Eventually, there was nothing left of the parent but a faded scaly skin, which split to allow the bright and lustrous infant to emerge.

In this process of self-consumption, the skills and memories of the parent dragon were inevitably lost, but the reproductive cycles of Yetzirah and Alziluth were staggered so that when each new Yetzirah emerged there would be a middle-aged Alziluth to teach it everything it would need to know—and *vice versa*. By this means all the wisdom that the two dragons accumulated during their wanderings in infinite space was carefully communicated from Yetzirah to Alziluth, and from Alziluth to Yetzirah by ceaseless repetition.

The vulnerability of their lore was recognized by both individuals. Each one knew that if a fatal accident were to befall the other its next clone-child would be born into a dire predicament of irredeemable ignorance. But this was not something that frightened them unduly because in all their travels they had never found any other creatures that were capable of killing dragons. Dragons were virtually invulnerable to harm, as befitted creatures that could navigate the void between the galaxies untroubled by hunger, patiently awaiting opportunities to draw marvelous nourishment from the excited light of exploding stars.

They knew, of course, that they did not remember everything that their previous selves had experienced, because they had forgotten their own origin, but they were confident that with every reincarnation the sum of their wisdom increased, and they saw no reason why they should not continue to increase their wisdom until the universe itself collapsed and died.

Alas for these hopes, the time came—as, perhaps, in the measureless reaches of eternity it was certain one day to come—when Yetzirah and Alziluth quarreled.

How the quarrel began is uncertain; it was some trivial matter of impoliteness that planted a tiny seed of resentment. But that seed once planted grew in the heart of whichever dragon accepted it, and led to a retaliatory impoliteness, which planted in its turn a second seed in the heart of the other; by the time either dragon became properly aware of what was happening, their hearts were already hardening against one another, and each was utterly convinced that the blame lay with the other.

And so the quarreling went on, and the rift between the two grew wider and wider, until each dragon in turn was drawn to commit an act that the other wrathfully decided to call "unforgivable".

They should have parted then, and gone their separate ways for a while (as perhaps their former selves had done before, although no such story had been handed down across the generations). Then, when the time came for one to lay an egg, it would surely have seen what a dire need there was for reconciliation, and it would have sought out the other—who must in the meantime have grown lonely and regretful—and proposed a new pact of eternal amity.

They did not part, however, and fell instead to fighting over the most delicious radiations of a particularly tasteful supernova...and as they roiled and raged in the luminous foam of that unfolding cosmic glory, the dragon Yetzirah wounded the dragon Alziluth most horribly with its savage teeth and claws.

When Yetzirah realized what its climactic fit of ill-temper had led it to do, its disappointment and self-loathing knew no bounds. For more than a century it tried everything within its power to discover a way to save Alziluth from death, but there was no salvation to be found. As with every other creature in the universe, a dragon's power to destroy is far greater than its power to heal.

So it was that after sickening for a very long time, Alziluth finally died.

Less than a planetary century thereafter, Yetzirah knew that the time had come to lay an egg, and it could not deny the demands of its inner nature. It swallowed the egg after the invariable fashion of its kind, and was consumed from within by a new Yetzirah. But that new Yetzirah was born into an awful loneliness, with no mentor to teach it the wisdom of the ages. In the absence of such assistance it grew to maturity not as a creature of vast intelligence and knowledge, but as a mere animal wandering aimlessly in the void, carelessly seeking out the luscious light of dying stars in response to its feeble appetites.

Ever thereafter, whenever it met other creatures, the dragon Yetzirah would fall upon them angrily, rending them with its fearsome teeth and claws, although it did not need their flesh for meat, nor had it any need at all to fear that they could hurt it. And while it rent them thus, it cried bitter and anguished tears—but it did not know why.

A SAINT'S PROGRESS

There were once as many accounts of the destruction of the wicked city of Is as there were active storytellers in Bretagne, although most of them vanished from human ken without ever being written down. Their contradictory profusion is hardly surprising, when one bears in mind that all but a few the witnesses to the event were drowned in the flood. Indeed, it is not impossible that all the city's inhabitants drowned, without exception, and that the individuals named as survivors in various versions of the tale are all fictitious, having been invented by storytellers to add a gloss of authority to their fancies.

The few things on which most surviving versions of the legend agree include the assertion that the king of Is at the time of the inundation was named Gradlon; that his daughter—sometimes named Dahut—was seduced by a foreign prince who might or might not have been the Devil in disguise, and persuaded to steal the key that operated the city's floodgates; that dire warnings were issued to the city's inhabitants to repent of their legendary wickedness, either by a ragged saint or the talking donkey on which he rode; and that the donkey contrived to carry a single survivor—sometimes Gradlon, sometimes the saint—to safety. In fact, none of these things can confidently be reckoned to be true, except for the interpolated observation that the wealthier inhabitants of Is were legendary for their wickedness—or, at the very least, for their decadence.

At the time of its inundation Is had no king, being merely a port in the province of Leonais, in the realm of Bretagne. Even its ancient dukedom had died out long before, although there was a madman living in a crumbling manor house some leagues away who styled himself the Duc d'Ys, employing the obsolete spelling of the city's name in the faint hope of making his imposture seem more plausible. Is was, however, exceptional among the great cities of Bretagne in having no single governor at all, being ruled instead by a council of seven wealthy merchants, who liked to style themselves the Merchant Princes of Is. Positions on this council were avidly sought and jealously defended, as were the alliances that formed temporary majorities in its decision-making; for this reason, very few of its members lived into old age and it was exceedingly rare for any of the to die from any other cause than murder.

At the time of the inundation, there was indeed a powerful member of this ruling committee named Gradlon, and he did have a daughter named Dahut, whose extraordinary powers of seduction he traded like any other commodity in which he dealt, for the purposes of making and sealing alliances. He also used her on occasion to tempt foreign visitors with whom he wished to establish profitable dealings, but none of them ever succeeded in seducing her affections away from her father or conquering her appetite for debauchery. The city did have floodgates, as any low-lying coastal city would, but they did not have to be opened to let in the inundation, which was the result of a tidal wave provoked by a subterranean earthquake, the first shock of which also lowered the land surface along a three-league stretch if coastline, somewhat after the fashion of the one that had previously drowned Alexandria and toppled its famous Pharos.

The matter of the saint is, however, more controversial. The conversion of Bretagne was long held to be one of the great triumphs of early Christendom, because there was nowhere else on the European continental landmass where paganism—in this case Druidism, or Bardic Mysticism—was more deeply rooted. One consequence of this struggle was that an unusually large number of saints were retrospectively created in celebration of the eventual victory, which could not be reckoned complete until the very eve of the Age of Chivalry, some eight hundred years after Christ's crucifixion.

Although Is, as a port city, was supposedly converted long before the remoter depths of the great forest of Leonais, and was nominally Christian for two centuries before its inundation, it seems likely that it still played host to covert Druidism at that time, and not only among the common people. Given this circumstance, it would not be at all surprising had there been dozens, or even hundreds, of would-be saints abroad in Is when the tidal wave struck, nor that many of them should be wandering the streets in rags crying "Repent, for the end is nigh!"—because that is, after all, the kind of thing that saints-in-waiting do.

More than one of these would-be saints probably followed his vocation with the aid of a donkey, and probably talked to the animal in question—although it seems much less probable that the donkey talked back. That phase of the legend does, therefore, have a certain ring of plausibility—except for the part in which the donkey is said to have carried a survivor to safety.

The only accounts of the inundation of Is that can really be considered trustworthy are those compiled by eye-witnesses who had high enough vantage-points inland to have seen the tidal wave strike. Only one of those, however, claimed to have been in Is within the previous few days, and to have been party to events there that might have formed the basis of the legend. This witness was a monk by the name of Winwaloe, who later became an abbot. That appointment was fortunate, in that it meant that he was not only able but felt compelled to write his story down and ensure that it would be copied. It was also unfortunate, in that his vocation led him to take a particular view of events preceding the disaster of which a secular reader—let alone a Bardic sympathizer—might be deeply skeptical. At any rate, the document survives today, doubtless having been copied many times over, as the only contemporary account of the destruction of Is.

Winwaloe's legend claims that he was educated by Saint Budoc on the "island" of Laurea, but that is a veiled reference to the story of Is, because Laurea was, in fact, a hill in the great forest of Leonais, which only became an island once, and very briefly, during the great inundation. It had originally had a different name and had been an important site of Druidic sacrifice—which was exactly why the Christians who came to Bretagne to convert its inhabitants built a monastery upon it.

The monastery of Laurea was deliberately equipped with an unusually tall bell-tower, whose roof commanded a view of a large sector of the forest and—in the remote distance—the city of Is. From its cold and breezy heights the Brothers of the order could down, albeit at a very shallow angle, on the city they considered to be the most wicked in the world, and surrender themselves completely to the voluptuous disapproval with which monks habitually displace other kinds of arousal.

As with any kind of voluptuousness, the disapproval of monks is often languid and inactive, but the stuff of which would-be saints are made is sterner by far. Saints-in-waiting never fail to engage the objects of their disapproval in battle—not literal battle, for monastic vows generally forbid the use of weapons, but other kinds of conquest no less fierce and furious.

History informs us that saints-to-be often leave powerful lords and princes alone, no matter how violent their petty armies become in that business of robbery which the powerful call taxation, and no matter how conclusively the lords and princes in question might compromise their chances of getting into Heaven by growing fat and rich, devoting themselves obsessively to the cruel pleasures of tyranny and the vain pursuits of luxury, and even turning, as the most corrupt of that kind often do, to the secret worship of forbidden gods. Budoc and his protégé Winwaloe were, however, not of that kind; they detested he merchant princes of Is, and were determined to act against them if the Lord would only grant them the means to do so.

In truth, Budoc knew little or nothing about the merchant princes of Is, never having had the opportunity to catch so much as a single glimpse of one. Rumor had, however, informed him that the most powerful of the seven was named Gradlon, who had very probably sold his soul to the Devil in exchange for his wealth, and that his daughter Dahut—who was possessed of unnatural beauty and unnatural appetites—would very likely make the same bargain as son as she became old enough, in law, to set her bloody thumb-print on a contract. Most of Budoc's unreliable informants told him that Dahut was already damned, by virtue of her numerous sins of the flesh, but a few suggested that she was only an unwitting pawn in her father's and the Devil's hands, and yet might be saved if only she could be assisted to see the light. If that could be achieved, the monastery's visitors suggested, then she might become a useful protectress of the city's many poor Christians, who were presently suffering persecution at a level that had rarely been experienced before, even in pagan Rome.

Budoc would dearly have liked to take on the task of saving Dahut himself, but he was already getting old, and he thought that the task was far more suited to a younger and more virile man—but a young and virile man who has had the advantage of an exceptionally fine teacher of a sort that he had always regretted not having had in his own youth. He therefore looked around for an apprentice, to whom he could rapidly teach everything he knew—which, fortunately, was not much—and in whom he could readily inspire the kind of dedication necessary to accomplish the task. The apprentice he selected was, of course, Winwaloe, who was little more than a youth.

Winwaloe was clear of eye, strong in wind and limb, and eager to learn. Budoc gave him a rapid course in all the disciplines of strictness, austerity and repression, with such awesome rigor that it only took him a matter of weeks to give the boy a near-absolute tyranny over his own flesh and a near-inflexible command of his own will. Budoc also taught him also the secret language of the sacred law and the awesome lexicon of banishment that conferred upon the Church's heroic exorcists the power to drive demons back to their hellish seats, thus cleansing the world of their filthy presence.

"I have never had occasion to use these formulas myself," Budoc told Winwaloe, "but I have no reason at all to doubt their efficacy, provided that the Lord approves of their deployment. Use them wisely, but use them with a will."

For a few more days thereafter, Budoc kept Winwaloe by his side, completing the work of shaping and refining him in body and mind, straitening his every thought within the provisions of divine law, until he was perfectly certain that he had made an instrument for the Lord far more powerful and considerably more skilled than he had been in his own younger days. Then, after fasting for two days, he prayed to the Lord for guidance as to what to do next.

In response to these prayers, Budoc was sent a dream, in which he saw the stern and stony face of the Lord, who said to him: "The city named Is harbors an evil out of all proportion to its relatively modest size. That city, personified in its wayward daughter Dahut, will provide the perfect test for the blade which you have forged in my name; it will temper him if he is sound, and shatter him if he is weak. Send him forth with a crucifix to reclaim Is for the cause of Christ, but warn him sternly lest his resolve be weakened by temptation."

Budoc was not surprised by any of this, which was exactly the instruction he had expected and hoped for, and he was delighted to have confirmation of his intentions direct from the Ultimate Source. He found a crucifix whose cross was carved from black ebony-wood and whose figure of Chris was fabricated in ivory, and he hung it around his acolyte's neck. He also gave the adolescent a stout walking-stick, very straight and plain, cut from the heartwood of a tall pine, and instructed him to use it as circumstances demanded and the Lord commanded. Then, without a tear in his eye or any other sign of affectionate feeling, Budoc pointed at the road to Is, and sent Winwaloe forth upon it.

* * * * * * *

The forest region that Winwaloe crossed on his way to the shore of the Great Ocean was sparsely populated, save for a narrow strip to either side of the road he was following, which extended far beyond Laurea in the direction of the place where Rennes now stands. There were enough good Christians distributed along the route to give him water and the occasional crust of bread while he made his way to the lush lowlands planted with the manifold crops of the region: turnips, beets, apples, cabbages and even a few fields of barley and wheat.

The walls of Is were not very high, but the vast palace in which the Merchant Princes met in council and conducted their business affairs had one high much higher tower that loomed above all the rest, black and forbidding. The sea could not be seen from any location inside the town wall, except for the actual quays surrounding the harbor; it was not often in the thoughts of many of those who had made their homes within that wall, who rarely went down to the docks or climbed up to the ramparts to look out at the source of the city's wealth. The Merchant Princes could, however, see the whole vast extent of the sea from their council-chamber.

The guardsmen at the Landward Gate had grown complacent in the ten long years since pirates had last attacked the city, and Winwaloe came unchallenged into its streets. One of the guards even consented to give him directions to the market-place when he asked where the best pace might be to catch a glimpse of Princess Dahut. He went immediately to the street beside the market-place that the guard had described, and there unrolled a rush-mat from which he could deliver sermons, when the time seemed ripe, and hear the confessions of anyone whose sins had become excessively burdensome. The rumor of his arrival passed through the streets quickly enough, but no crowd gathered about his mat, curious to hear what he had to say. Indeed, the only person who spoke to him on is first day in the city, apart from the guard at the gate, was the priest of the parish in which he had laid out his mat, who told him that his presence was quite unnecessary and definitely unwelcome.

"I am the good shepherd responsible for this particular flock," the priest assured him, "and I have no need of any witchfinder or exorcist to assist me in my work."

"How frequently does Princess Dahut pass by here?" Winwaloe asked, mildly.

"Far too frequently," was the only reply he received.

Several days went by without Winwaloe being able to catch a glimpse of Princess Dahut, but he did manage to beg enough bread and water from passers-by to take the edge of his hunger and thirst, in spite of the vituperations of the market traders and the fact that the parish priest had very ostentatiously told his flock at Sunday mass to ignore him. Finally, he felt that the time was ripe for him to deliver a sermon.

No crowd gathered before Winwaloe spoke, and few passers-by paused while he was speaking, but he preached regardless, extolling the virtues of stern self-discipline and self-restraint. It is highly probable that no one took the slightest notice of anything he said, but his declamatory pose showed off his strength and handsomeness to good effect, and those qualities seemed all the more intriguing by virtue of the cold austerity of his manner and speech. No one asked him to serve as a confessor, but a few devout individuals took the trouble to bring him news of the many evils that were said to be abroad in the town—rumors of children being kidnapped and murdered so that their innocent blood might be used in satanic rituals; rumors of lewd displays and dread perversions practiced within the Merchant Princes' palace; rumors of demonic possessions and animal familiars. It was the people who brought him such tales who also sometimes brought him half a loaf of bread and pitcher of water, as if to reward him for hearing their complaints.

The more he heard of what the people of Is had to tell him, the more Winwaloe felt a sickening horror creeping upon him. He had little or no understanding of the ways in which rumors often become exaggerated by repetition, for his sheltered life had given him no opportunity to see how even the least offensive of individuals lusts after lurid gossip, and increases it when she passes it on. He heard what was said about Gradlon of Is and his gaudy daughter Dahut without realizing that the tales had been reinvented a hundred times over in the hope of keeping them fresh, and he believed every word of what he was told.

By nightfall on his fifth day in Is, Winwaloe was resolved to bring down the wrath of the Lord upon the city, in the fullest measure which his own virtue and determination might contrive. When he laid himself down upon his mat that night, however, to offer up his prayers and beg for guidance from the Lord, he initially found only darkness and confusion in his mind. Although he strove as mightily as he could to find enlightenment with his inner eye, no guiding vision came. It was not until the criers called the hour after midnight, and all was still in the streets, that a messenger came looking for him: a gold-haired boy in a white tunic, who asked that Winwaloe follow him.

Winwaloe did follow the mysterious child, who led him through the winding alleys behind the street alongside the market-place to an arched doorway in a tall, forbidding wall. Beyond the doorway there were dim-lit labyrinthine corridors and spiral flights of stairs, which turned him around in his course so many times that he felt sure that he would never be able retrace his steps without a guide.

Eventually, the messenger brought him into an apartment that was much more brightly lit than the corridors. There, lying on a crimson couch, was a woman no older than himself. Her hair was black, but sleek enough to glitter as it caught the light. Her brown eyes were no less lustrous. Her lips were glossed with crimson, so that all her features seemed radiant. There was incense burning in the room, and the intoxicating vapors teased the mucous membranes of Winwaloe's nose.

"I hear that you have been asking for me," the woman said, in a voice that was low and honey-sweet. "I am sorry that I have not been to the market these last few days, but my father has had need of me. In any case, what I heard about you provoked me to summon you here instead of coming to look at you on your mat. Your name is Winwaloe, is it not?"

"And yours, I presume, is Dahut," the adolescent replied. "I have heard a great deal about you."

"Nothing good, I dare say," the princess said, with a sigh. "But that is not my fault; I have little control over what people think of me or say about me."

"That's true," Winwaloe admitted, simultaneously answering her tacit question and accepting her excuse. "There is still time to repent your wicked ways and become a true follower of Christ. I have come to assist you with the salvation of your soul."

She laughed at that, and said: "I'm sure that you'll do your best—but I doubt that my father would approve, and I can't honestly say that I've ever had any strong desire to be saved. Still, I've been told that you're a handsome fellow when you preach, and I'd like to see it. May I ask something is return, though, before you begin preaching?"

"What is it?" Winwaloe asked, warily.

"Only that you might look at me and listen to me for as long as I have been required to look at you and listen to you."

"Do you intend to preach a satanic sermon to me?" Winwaloe asked.

"Perhaps," Dahut replied. "Are you so terrified of being the convert rather than the converter that you dare not hear such a thing?"

"Oh no," said Winwaloe. "I have no fear of the Devil's sophistry. My master Budoc has taught me well. Not only do I agree to your terms, but I will allow you to take the first turn, if you wish. That way, you can determine the time that you will be promising to grant to me."

"That's very kind of you," Dahut said, "and I accept your offer gladly. I'm not much of a sermonizer, though, for I've always believed that actions speak louder than words. Perhaps I might dance for you instead of preaching verbally?"

"Certainly," Winwaloe replied. "There is nothing in our agreement that forbids movement."

Dahut danced, for what seemed like an eternity—although it was actually no more than half an hour, according to the graded candle that the princess had set to measure her performance. She was accompanied by two musicians, one on a lute and one on a tambour, but she provided extra embellishments with the aid of Turkish finger-cymbals. She was a very fine dancer, and the serpentine sinuousness of her movements gave the impression that the silken garments she was wearing were actually polished scales.

When she had finished her dance, she said: "Imagine, if you can, Winwaloe, what pleasures you might find in my flesh, if only you had the wit to seek them out. Behold me, son of man, and ask whose face you would rather see in your dreams, whenever the burden of wakefulness is lifted from your soul: Christ's as it was on the cross, or mine?"

Winwaloe's immediate reply to this was to take out the crucifix he wore on his breast and study the face of the ivory Christ. "Yours is very pretty," he admitted, "but I prefer Christ's. Will you hear me now?"

She laughed, and said: "Of course I will. I always honor my promises, when I have the freedom to do so. There are so many instances, alas, when I do not, that I am always eager to seize the remaining opportunities."

Winwaloe preached then, with no accompaniment but his own expressive gestures. He lauded the virtue of self-discipline and self-restraint, as usual, but added further homilies on the topics of humility, chastity, charity and faith.

When he had finished, Dahut said: "That too was a dance of sorts, and as a connoisseur of dancing, I thought it rather fine."

"If you would like to confess your sins," Winwaloe said, "I am ready to hear your confession, and am empowered to grant you absolution if you are truly repentant."

"That is very kind of you," Dahut replied. "Yes, I think it might be rather amusing to confess my sins."

She proceeded to do so; it took a good deal longer than her dance had taken, but it omitted many of the more lurid details of the tales that Winwaloe had been told in the street beside the marketplace.

"You have made no mention of diabolical influence," he pointed out, obligingly, when the well of secrets finally began to run dry. "You seem to have committed a great many abominable crimes against God's law and your fellow men alike, and I am glad to hear that you did so many of them unwillingly, in response to your father's demands, but you have not said anything about your father's pact with the Devil and its unfortunate consequences for you."

Dahut seemed surprised by that. "I could easily believe that my father might be in league with the Devil," she said, "but I know very well that he does not believe in any such individual—and nor do I. He commits his own sins, and directs mine, in the name of business and political authority."

"The Devil has many disguises," Winwaloe admitted, judiciously, "And those who have signed his awful pact often have the fact blanked from their memory. Nevertheless, I do not believe that you have signed any such pact, as yet, and I am certain that you can be absolved of our sins, provided that you are truly repentant of them all, and will promise to do everything in your power to resist temptation in future."

"I'm sorry," Dahut said, "but I can't do that."

"Why not?" Winwaloe asked.

"Firstly, because I certainly do not repent all of them, and secondly—although it might be reckoned a mere corollary point—I certainly cannot promise always to resist temptation in the future. Those sins which I do not repent, I fully intend to repeat, as often as I can, while they still give me pleasure. Indeed, if there are any pleasures that I have not yet had the opportunity to savor, I hope with all my heart eventually to obtain their savor."

"That is very foolish, Princess" Winwaloe said. "An attitude of that sort can only lead to traffic with demons."

"Well," said Dahut, shrugging her shoulders, "if such traffic can bring me ecstasy, at little enough cost, it would merely be good business to involve myself in it. In my opinion, it is pleasure, not law—whether the law in question is Man's or God's—that is the best measure of the things of this world. Indeed I incline to the view that where there is pleasure, there can be no crime, and where there is no possibility of pleasure, there can be no virtue. Are you quite sure, Winwaloe, that you would not like to reconsider my previous offer? It is by far the best bargain that will ever be presented to you?"

Winwaloe had to cast his mind back over the conversation to be sure that he had never been made any specific offer—but when he had, he conceived a strong suspicion of what it was that she meant. "Are you quite sure, Princess Dahut," he riposted, "that you would not like to reconsider mine? It is by far the best that you will ever receive?"

She laughed again, with seemingly sincere delight.

"You might not know it now, Winwaloe," she said, "but when you sleep, your dreams will surely tell you a higher truth than your sullen God would like you to hear."

"Impossible," said Winwaloe, confidently.

It seemed then that something struck him down from behind.

When he woke up again, quite unable to guess how long he had been unconscious, he was lying on his mat beneath the open sky, in the street beside the deserted market-place.

Was it a dream? he wondered—but he decided that it could not have been a dream. He stretched himself out upon his mat, and called upon the Lord to give him strength. And when, some time afterwards, he fell asleep, that sleep was quite untroubled by dreams.

In the morning, men-at-arms came to Winwaloe's mat. They seized him in the name of Prince Gradlon, and conveyed him through the web of alleyways behind the street to a postern gate in the wall of the palace. Once inside, they took him swiftly to the dungeons, where they cast him through a hole in the floor into a noisome and filthy pit, and threw his walking-stick in after him. When he protested this treatment, they replied that the laws of Is reckoned it as dire an offence to hear treason as it was to speak it, and that he was guilty of both. They put a large flat stone over the mouth of the oubliette to seal him in, and left him in darkness.

This, Winwaloe knew, was the beginning of his martyrdom, and also his triumph. The Lord had allowed the servants of Satan to cast him down in order that he might rise again, in due course, to serve as His instrument of justice. With this in mind, he embraced the grimy stones of his prison, and began to chant the prayers that he had long been used to sing in the monastery of Laurea.

"Make these stones live, Lord, in order that they might free me!" he implored. "Make the earth itself rise up against those who have polluted it!"

For three days and three nights Winwaloe did nothing but pray. His captors brought him neither food nor water, but he did not care; there was a different nourishment in the process of digestion within his soul.

Finally, when the time was ripe, Winwaloe began to deploy the formulas that Budioc had taught him. He pronounced an anathema upon wicked souls of the city of Is, and an exorcism upon its countless demons. As he did so, he felt the crucifix upon his breast grow hot and bright. It seemed to him that the dark pit was suddenly filled with the cold and silver light of God's law, and he heard a voice saying to him: "Climb up quickly, if you can, Winwaloe. It's time to flee the city, else my father will surely have you killed."

It seemed to Winwaloe then that his long walking-staff began to throb with power. He raised it up above his head, into the opening through which the dazzling light was pouring, and he heard someone say: "Grab hold of that, you fools, and pull him up, or I'll have your heads." And it seemed to him that he rose up into the air, carried aloft by his staff, into the light. Later, when he touched it to a stone wall, it seemed to him that the stone simply peeled away, splitting the wall asunder to make a path for him, which led him away from the palace of Is towards the gate through which he had entered it. As he began to march along the road that lay before him, he began to murmur a new and triumphant prayer, which grew louder and louder as the voices of a phantom choir joined in.

Twice, as he moved the streets of the city, he was challenged by men-at-arms with halberds and swords, who asked him where he was going—but he only said: "Away from here! Away from accursed Is, forever!" Then he whirled his staff about above his head, and they fell back, awed by the power flowing from its ends. The power did not break their weapons or drive them to their knees, because they were already numbered among the damned; it simply left them to their fate.

"I am the Lord's instrument!" Winwaloe shouted, between the choruses of his continuing prayer. "Temptation has not touched me, and passion has no place in my heart! I am the Lord' instrument, and I have come to deliver His retribution against the servants of Satan!"

That was when the demons which held Is hostage attacked him with all their might. A strange host of shadows assailed him, but their intangible talons, fangs and deadly stings could no more prick him than the clumsy weapons of the soldiers had been able to do. His crucifix burned and his staff twirled, and the monstrous shadows were swept into whirlpools in the air, which denied them their horrid aspect and swallowed them up entire.

"Demons, loose your hold upon this place!" he chanted, swollen with honest pride in his virtue and his power. "Evil, begone! I am the instrument of the Lord and no resistance is possible! God's law reigns here now, and will not be denied!"

Although he was heading in the opposite direction, Winwaloe cast his mind back to the palace of the Merchant Princes, and to Dahut's apartments. She had suggested to him that he would see her in his dreams, but she was wide awake when she became aware of his miraculous presence, which outshone the entire riot of color formed by tapestries, curtains, sofas and ornaments. The color was blasted from cushions and graven images alike by the cold white light of God's law; crystal shattered everywhere, spilling dark red wine to stain the floor.

Somewhere in the whirlwind of righteous wrath there was a sound of screaming, but Winwaloe saw nothing, so intense was the pitch of his excitement. His voice repeated the syllables of power contained in the formulas that Budoc had taught him, and the very earth awoke, as he had requested it should, to do the bidding of the Lord.

"Jesu! Jesu! Jesu!" Winwaloe cried, with a rapture akin to possession, thrilling to the icy coldness of his unbreakable resolve.

* * * * * * *

Much later, having returned to Laurea, Winwaloe took Budoc up to the roof of the bell-tower in order to explain what he had done.

"I heard Princess Dahut's confession," he told his superior, "but she would not repent. She had already signed the Devil's pact in her blood, and there was nothing to be done for her. I had no alternative."

He looked at the horizon where Is was, and pointed at the highest tower of the palace of the Merchant Princes, at the platform where sentries were posted to watch the silver ribbon of the sea's horizon for the white sails of pirate ships.

No sentry was on that rampart now, but the sorceress Dahut was there. She stumbled as he caught sight of her, as if his vision were as powerful as a fist or a squall of wind. She had no weapon in her hand, nor any demonic power in her eyes. She no longer shone with her unnatural glamour, and she had lost the natural bloom of youth along with her stolen glory. She was dull now, and helpless.

"Can you see her?" Winwaloe said to Budoc.

"Who?" the abbot replied. "If there were anyone there, we could not see anything at this distance but tiny dots."

"I can see better than that," Winwaloe assured him. "I can also make myself heard." Addressing himself to Dahut, he said: "See what all your temptations have come to, my pretty princess! How feeble were your charms, against the strength of the Lord! Did you really think that you could awaken lust in a man like me, who had the future Saint Budoc to teach me and Christ for my inspiration? Learn, then, how impotent Satan is against a true will and a stern soul!"

When she looked back at him, astonished to see him so clearly at such an enormous distance, he saw in her eyes that she had, indeed, learned what folly it had been to oppose his sermon so lightly with laughter and temptation. He saw that she knew pain now, as well as pleasure, and knew which was the stronger in the world, and what price was ordained by the Lord for the luxurious and the lascivious to pay.

She did not seek for a second time to awaken his passion with the promise of her flesh. Instead, she begged him for his help, pleading with him to save her life—to save her from the very demonic forces that she had sought to enjoy and command.

"I will be whatever you want me to be," she said. "I will do whatever penance you demand. Only save me from the vengeance of the people, and the wrath of the demons with which I made treaties. Only save me, now that you have destroyed all that I had and all that I loved."

Then, while Winwaloe stared at her, sternly, she fell upon her knees, and put her arms across her bosom, as if she were trying to hide within herself from everything that was outside her.

Winwaloe looked down at her—and suddenly, because he could not help himself, he felt a pang of pity. The staff that had lifted him out of the dungeon suddenly became heavy in his hand, as though it were only made of wood. The crucifix upon his chest ceased to burn with righteous fire, and became as heavy as a dead stone. The grandiose incantation that had possessed his mind and made him more than human faded, in his imagination, to a mere plaintive echo. Still, he could not help himself.

He looked at the frail woman who had been the sorceress Dahut, and saw through the dullness of her presence the brightness of what she had earlier been. Lust did not trouble him, so well had Budoc taught him what a monk must know and what a monk must be— but pity, in spite of all that he had done, he had not even begun to conquer. The temptation to lust he had resisted, but he had not properly learned that that there were other temptations that might touch an unwary heart.

Winwaloe knew that the test of worthiness that had tried his power against the might of Is's demons was not yet done; as a sword of justice he was not yet tempered, and might yet break. He opened his mouth to speak to the stricken Dahut, but, for a fateful moment, he did not know what to say. When he did speak, it was to damn himself, for what he said was: "Don't despair, Princess. Perhaps there is forgiveness in the world, even for the unrepentant."

He looked away towards the west then, to hide the feeling that had cracked the ice in his soul from Budoc, who had labored so long and heart to set it there.

What he saw made him catch his breath in fearful surprise.

He saw the tidal wave surge upon Is, and the great forest of Leonais.

In the fields and the farmhouses of the coastal strip, people were hurrying back and forth in a belated attempt to save what they could, whether it might be horses, cattle or household goods. It did not matter; there was no escape, except for a few flocks of geese.

Winwaloe wanted to call out to the panic-stricken people, to tell them that there was no need for them to flee, because he had cleansed the city of evil, and they were Heaven-bound—but when he opened his mouth, he found that he had no voice.

When he looked at the forest surrounding Laurea, he saw that it had become an island. Everywhere else, from horizon to horizon, the great grey waves were eating up the land that the sad cold sea had given, for a little while, to the charge and use of man.

"But I shall be canonized as a saint, one day," he whispered, too faintly for Budoc to hear.

And he was.

MENS SANA IN CORPORE SANO

We had to take that particular sales pitch on to the road because everyone had stopped believing in anything they saw on TV or in any other kind of virtual reality. Appearances could so easily be faked; we had to approach people in the flesh, and show them what we could do to the flesh, in such a way that they could feel the power and the sweat, or they never would have taken us seriously. We had to go on to the stages and into the lecture-rooms.

If there'd been any churches left we'd have gone into them too, because ours was an honest-to-God crusade, a way to salvation, a pathway to Heavenly Bliss. Our work always is; that's the kind of people we are.

Don't think it was easy, just because we were selling something every man jack of them had ardently desired all his life, something every one of their august forefathers had yearned after for centuries, something so very dear to the innermost tropisms of the human heart that every red-blooded male who ever stood to attention would have sold his soul for half as much. Oh no! If you think that, you don't understand human psychology, and if you can't understand human psychology you can't begin to understand marketing.

If you stand on a street-corner offering to swap thousand-dollar bills for twenties you'll get no takers, because nobody will believe they're real. It's really quite difficult to do good in the world.

Paradoxical as it may seem, sellers of perfection have to promise that it will cost you blood, sweat and tears, or no one will take them seriously. You can sell blood, sweat, tears and trickery, but you can't sell unadulterated trickery. "You too can have a body like mine," Charles Atlas used to say (and made millions saying it), "but only if you learn the artistry of dynamic tension, and work at it." The steroid-sellers had a very similar pitch; in order to get the most out of the boosters you had to pump a lot of iron.

They say that Marlon Brando was a Charlie Atlas fan. Cynics suggested that his addiction to dynamic tension was what led him to fall prey to fat and foul temper, but cynics make lousy marketing men. The lesson to be learned from long-dead Marlon, as far as we were concerned, was that no man had ever been able to be content with beauty, genius and boundless charisma, if he thought he could have a body like a demigod too.

Our models really were demigods, and our demonstrations set out to prove the fact. We used to let the members of the audience come up and stick knives in them—their own knives, of course, so they'd be confident it wasn't any kind of conjuring trick—to show off the models' pain-control and healing ability. Some of the kids would bring ancient cut-throat razors, or wicked daggers with barbs and serrated edges, or stilettos, which they tried to thrust in between the ribs slap bang at the heart.

They couldn't actually get through to the heart, of course. The enhanced intercostals were so powerfully-armored that they could stop bullets—the kind of bullets we had then, that is. We demonstrated that, too, but not to the general public; some pitches we had to save for special clients, and the military market is a such a prolific cash cow that we figured that we ought to take special care with it. It would have been bad tactics to let anyone but the military test our models to destruction, or anywhere near destruction.

We let the public play with fire too, but only trivial stuff like candles and red hot pokers—no blowtorches or Molotov cocktails. The models weren't fussed; it was a macho thing with them to push the pain-control facility to its limit, and the most advanced among them claimed to find a unique pleasure in modified burning sensations. We had to careful to avoid gross-out, though. Knife-wounds that close up again under the authority of will-power are one thing; charred flesh is another, even after it starts to turn pink again.

We did all the gymnastic routines and the weightlifting, of course, but only because it was expected. It didn't make a damn of difference to the sales pitch; people had grown far too accustomed to seeing stunts of that kind in movies and VR-tapes, and even though they knew full well that the movie versions all done with camera-cunning they still found it tedious when it was repeated live and honest. It was the hands-on business with the knives and the branding-irons that really turned the punters on. By the time they'd seen our guys laughing off the deep pricks and the hot licks they were avid to be sold.

For reasons I've already made clear, though, we had to make it seem as if they weren't getting it all for nothing.

"Of course," we told them, although there was no *of course* about it, "you have to make the effort to learn the art of pain-control, and you have to take the time to train the muscles properly. Somatic reinforcement and nanotech CNS-enhancement only put the systems in place. You don't have any instinctive knowledge of how to use the resources; you don't take to it naturally, the way you take to breathing and sleeping. You can become men like gods, but you have to be *self-made* men like gods."

Flattery will get you almost anywhere. Whatever a man will pay for perfection, he'll pay double for the illusion that the credit is all his. And we don't, of course, have any instinctive knowledge of how to use somatically-reinforced flesh decked out with add-on nerve-endings; we really do have to learn to use such things. It's just that the learning process is absolutely automatic, as close as you'll ever get to classical conditioning—which is exactly what you'd expect, given that pain is the bottom line of avoidance-conditioning. Once the control apparatus was in place, it refined itself—but because the punters were conscious of the rapid improvement they thought they were doing it themselves, and felt fully entitled to be proud of their facility.

The tours were grueling, but we had a lot of fun. After all, we weren't just making a fortune—we were helping mankind through the next phase of his evolution, building the Earthly Paradise, selling the Elixir of Life itself.

We really believed that. In my heart of hearts, I still do.

There was opposition, of course.

"Something's bound to go wrong," the pessimists wailed. "We don't know enough about the long-term side-effects. Steroids caused systemic stress, uncontrollable outbursts of aggression, sterility; these new body-building technologies are sure throw up problems of their own. Tampering with nature always leads to disaster." As if the whole history of human civilization weren't a glorious tale of tampering with nature leading triumphantly to transcendence!

The pessimists were right, of course, to some extent. The virtual abolition of pain meant that its warning function was lost along with the inconvenience, but that didn't matter a damn as long as we could cure all the cancers and infections that threatened to riot.

"The trouble with ideals of perfection," the skeptics slyly suggested, "is that once they're common property they lose their meaning. What men want isn't huge muscles and awesome powers of endurance, it's to outshine their competitors, their presumed rivals in the struggle for the esteem of others—whose basic yardstick is, of necessity, the esteem of women. If everybody is physically perfect, some other kind of discrimination will come to the fore."

The skeptics were right too, after a fashion, but that didn't matter a damn either. Wimps and weaklings didn't become suddenly fashionable; it was just that when everyone had become a demigod there remained a vacuum of demand for other, newer kinds of glamour. We certainly didn't mind that; the marketing man's greatest consolation is the knowledge that, however successful his current campaign is, there'll always be another to move on to.

"This business will take sexual politics back a hundred years," the feminist ecofreaks complained. "Women who claim the benefits that these new technologies offer will be penalized because men still prefer waif-like shrinking violets. In the meantime, men will be pushed even further into the rituals of masculinity whose fallout is devastating the planet. Unless men's attitudes change, this macho flesh-fetishism will simply add to the confusion that women already suffer and the forces that threaten to destroy all life on earth."

All of that was true enough, as far as it went, because it had always been true. It wasn't our fault that the pattern of demand had these glitches built in; we only reflected an imbalance that was already there—and the only hope the feminists and the ecofreaks have of ever getting rid of those problematic attitudes lies with people like us: marketing men! We're the only people who have the tools with which to begin the job of dismantling attitudes and building them anew....but in those days the tools we had for rebuilding flesh were far more effective and much simpler to use.

The opposition didn't stop there, of course, but that was the bulk of it. Some foxes simply can't stop protesting that the grapes must be sour, even when technology brings them within easy reach. But if there wasn't any opposition, there wouldn't be nearly as much need for marketing men. We didn't mind the opposition; it didn't cause us any pain. We appreciated a challenge as much as the next man—probably far more!

I was sorry when the great campaign was over. I still miss those heady days when we were really at the cutting edge of things (pun intended!), pushing back the frontiers of human experience. We really did change the world, maybe more than any marketing men had contrived to do since the days of the prophets and their ardent disciples.

We never got due credit for what we did. Afterwards, people looked back and said "Well, anyone could sell a product like *that*"—the difficulties just weren't obvious in retrospect. As soon as every-one has something, they take it for granted. They can't imagine be-ing without it, and can't understand how anyone might have to be persuaded to take it on. Things that we take for granted always come to seem trivial, no matter how vital a contribution they made to hu-man progress. The guy who invented the wheel wouldn't be a hero even if we knew his name. "Anyone could have thought of *that*," people would say. The guy who sold the wheel to the masses wouldn't even be a candidate for heroism, even though he'd have faced the same battery of criticism from pessimists, skeptics and en-trenched vested interests.

So why aren't we in Heaven yet?

I suppose, at the end of the day, you could say that we didn't really deliver on our promises. The souped-up muscles work just fine, of course, and the CNS-augment systems just keep getting slicker and slicker, but the credit for that goes to the scientists. What we added in was the dream. That's the one real product that market-ing men have, when you get down to the nitty-gritty. We weren't really selling the solid goods; they really did sell themselves, once we'd eased the way for them. What we were selling was the glamour that went with the goods.

What we were selling was demigodhood—and I suppose that all the while we were selling it we knew, deep down, that the skeptics would catch up with us eventually, because the skeptics always do. In the end, every marketing campaign—even the most successful—comes to grief.

That pun's intended too. Grief is the very essence of the failure of our crusade. The customers bought great new bodies, but they never attained perfection or salvation. Heavenly bliss remained stubbornly out of reach—because of grief.

Every gardener and agriculturalist knows about the law of limiting factors. A plant needs all kinds of things to grow: space, light, supportive soil, water, and a hundred different nutrients and minerals. Whichever one is in shortest supply, relatively speaking, becomes the factor limiting the growth of the plant—but every time you figure out what the limiting factor is, and make sure that it's in abundant supply, something else takes over its role.

There's always a limiting factor; even if you can assure an abundant supply of everything the plant needs from its external environment, it can't and won't grow infinitely because it has its own limiting factors inscribed in its genes and translated in its flesh. It's the same with people. No matter how much they have, or how constructively they're remade, there's always a limiting factor. Every time we answer what seems to be the most fundamental craving, the sharpest of needs, we just make space for another.

We sold our customers strength and freedom from physical pain—and however confused our female clients were about the mechanics of physical glamour, they were in no doubt at all about the benefits of freedom from pain—but, in so doing, we opened unprecedented scope for all the kinds of anguish that weren't physical. We blocked the ravages of true pain, and gave an unprecedented boost to the wellsprings of malice, melancholy and misery.

They say that the sum of human unhappiness has never been greater than it is today. Sometimes they say it wonderingly, as if it beggars belief, but it shouldn't be a surprise. And after all, it doesn't really matter that envy, hatred and wrath are running riot in today's world, given that we have the resilience to cope with all but the very worst effects. When you get right down to it, we don't really need to be sensitive to people's needs and desires any more, now that they're big enough and tough enough to take more or less anything we can hand out.

Anyhow, it's all just a matter of adaptation. It'll all work out in the end. Wars come and wars go, and sometimes it really is darkest just before the dawn. Take my word for it.

It helps, of course, if you have a sense of humor—or at least a sense of irony. "Man that is born of a woman hath but a short time to live, and is full of misery," we used to say in our prayers, not realizing how much fuller he might be if he had a longer time to live, and the strength to stand fast against all the slings and arrows of outrageous fortune. Who would ever have thought, back in the olden days, that people could be as perversely downhearted as they are now? The people who made up the myths had their heads screwed on, though—their demigods spent all their time fighting and being miserable, didn't they?

Mind you, we're not all downhearted, are we? I'm not. But then, I'm a marketing man, and every marketing man is a professional optimist. To me, and men like me, the human condition is an ever-evolving challenge, and there's nothing we like better than a challenge. Men of my kind are always looking forward to the next crusade, the next road to salvation, the next recipe for Heavenly Bliss.

And the good news is that we've found it—again!

It's something else, of course, that we've been searching for since time immemorial—something that will do for the mind what somatic reinforcement and CNS-augmentation did for the body. It's the ultimate psychotropic cocktail: the perfect tranquilizer; the ultimate euphoric; absolute and ecstatic calm of mind.

I know it won't be easy to sell, because everyone's heard it all before, a million times over, but we have the products, we have the skills and we have the guts to do it. The pessimists will talk about backlash effects and withdrawal symptoms and disrupted brain chemistry and possible mutagenic side-effects. The skeptics will argue that bliss might be a nice place to go for a holiday but that no sane person could want to live there and that the world would fall apart if people did. There'll be others joining in the chorus of disapproval, and the customers will need to be persuaded that they can take credit for the results themselves, that they're the true architects of their reward—but we can take care of all that and more.

It'll take ingenuity. After all, it's not as if we can just parade a bunch of models on a stage and invite the public to get their knives out. This is a whole new ball game—but we can play it. Where there's a will there's a whole flock of people avid to inherit.

And afterwards?

Afterwards, everything in the garden will be rosy. I really believe that this campaign can complete a transformation that the last one left half-finished; we'll have the *mens sana* to go with the *corpore sano*. I'm not saying that the new psychotropic revolution will put an end to the great riot of recklessness, but I'm pretty sure that it will stop people worrying about it as much as they do now. I don't know about malice, but melancholy and misery will be things of the past. This stuff will let us take things in our stride. Believe me, when we've sold this to the world, no one will give a damn about anything.

And after that? What will the next limiting factor be?

Well, we can only fight one crusade at a time. But there *will be* an afterwards, because the law of limiting factors says so. There's always a limiting factor, as long as something's alive and growing— and we're certainly alive and growing, aren't we? But don't cheer up just yet. Stay miserable just a little while longer. We'll be with you just as soon as we can, and we'll have the answer to your fondest dreams.

After all, that's our job—and our vocation. How could you possibly get by without us? Why would you ever want to?

BLACK NECTAR

When the great city of Is and part of the vast forest of Leonais were swallowed up by the flood that devastated the coast of Bretagne, a dozen smaller towns and half a hundred villages were also obliterated. Some were totally forgotten, and a few others remembered in name only. A few of the names that lingered in the memory of the people of Leonais did so because they had enjoyed an evil reputation and routinely featured in the kind of tales that people tell around the hearth on the eves of winter feasts, when talk inevitably turns to witches, korrigans, tailless cats and the like. One such town was Fourquevaux, which was situated to the east of Is, in the margin between the edge of the forest and the dunes.

Fourquevaux was a prosperous town, by the standards of the region, its inhabitants including numerous refugees from Is, who had found it politic to export their wealth from the city lest the secret police working for the Merchant Princes should somehow convince themselves that it might be ill-gotten. Such men invariably lived ostentatiously respectable lives, as retired bandits inevitably like to do, and frequently devoted themselves to the arts, as all men tend to do when they need not work for their living and must find some other way to occupy their time and minds. It was considered exceedingly impolite in Fourquevaux for any man to ask questions of his neighbors, especially regarding their activities in advance of settling there, and it was often said—especially in the market square—that the only thing anyone needed to know about any other was whether he settled his debts reliably.

Although the coast to either side of Is was, in the main, very gently sloped, it was not devoid of rocky outcrops, some of which still survive as tiny islands or reefs that pose a grave danger to ships at low tide. A group of such crags, known as the Devil's Claws, was situated to the north of Fourquevaux, forming a sort of natural defense against invasion from the sea—whose protection had doubtless encouraged the founding of the town in more primitive and barbarous days. These crags provided nesting-sites for numerous seabirds, including some gull species that rarely nested in the region, while the nearby marshes played host to an unusually rich selection of waders. Had the science of ornithology existed in the days before the Great Flood, Fourquevaux would undoubtedly have been one of the best locations in Bretagne to pursue that study, but that pastime was as yet uninvented, and the local people were more likely to regard the multitudinous birds as vermin, since they were not considered edible. Even so, idlers and tattletales sometimes reported that firebirds occasionally nested in the Devil's Claws, and that even larger and more mysterious birds often visited them by night, especially in the dark of the moon.

Although ornithology was unknown in Bretagne before the Great Flood, horticulture was not. Indeed, the cultivation of beautiful and exotic flower-gardens was among the arts of which the leisured classes of Fourquevaux were fondest. It was by no means extraordinary, if rumor can be believed at such a distance of time, for its wealthiest citizens to become quite obsessive about the cultivation of rare and special flowers. The lower orders, inevitably, tended to mock such affectations, and always referred to such men in rather scornful terms as "gardeners", but there is nothing as eternal as envy, which survives all natural disasters unscathed.

Although the people of Fourquevaux were as orthodox in their Christianity as everyone else in Bretagne, the dark tales that gave the town its reputation inevitably alleged that other kinds of worship were conducted there in secret. It is nowadays widely accepted that the last remnants of Druidism had not died out before the drowning of Is—indeed, the credulous still argue that it was for exactly that reason that the good Lord permitted the destruction of the city and its environs—and it is sometimes suggested that the aspects of Druidism that were condemned most enthusiastically by Rome's missionaries as Devil-worship were practiced with a particular passion there, by way of defiance of the Church's kindly way with heretics.

Nowadays, of course, there are also nostalgic apologists for Druidism, who claim that Druids were just as horrified by demon-worship as Christians are, and that if anyone in Is or its environs ever did sell his soul to some dark entity whose nature no one any longer knows and few would care to contemplate, he did so with no more encouragement from the Old Religion than from the New Testament.

* * * * * * *

Philippe Lekain had known Armand Kardan since boyhood, and yet—as was often the way of things in Fourquevaux—had never really *known* him. Although their fathers were both respectable corn-chandlers, sufficiently alike in their habits and opinions to pass for brothers, Philippe and Armand were very different. Whereas the former strived always to follow convention and to fit in with the society of his peers, the latter tended to set himself apart, finding anything ordinary dull. Armand came to fancy himself an artist of sorts at an unusually early age, although he was equally unskilled as a painter, a poet and a gardener. Philippe, for his part, often suspected that his friend's "art" was simply an ability to see the world from a strange angle, from which it seemed more magical and more malign; Armand was certainly attracted by all things unusual and arcane.

With the aid of this tilted perception, Armand might easily have gone into the Church, but his parents would not hear of such a thing, and he excused himself from going against their wishes—and hence excising himself from his father's will—by declaring that the monks and priests of Fourquevaux were, in any case, a poor and shabby lot, far less virtuous than they claimed to be. Had he lived in an earlier era, he sometimes said—perhaps by way of shocking his father and his friend—he would rather have trained as a Bard or learned the secret rituals of the golden sickle.

Such affectations embarrassed his family somewhat, but Armand saved himself from total disgrace by working hard to master the arts of reading, writing and arithmetic, which his illiterate father commended on the grounds that they would be very useful to a man in trade. Armand had no intention of employing these arts in such a vulgar manner, however; his true ambition was to entertain himself with books of a questionable character, and seek therein the secrets of arcane knowledge.

The Kardan house was three stories high, and set upon the ridge of a small hillock situated to the west of the town, outside the line of the ancient, long-cannibalized rampart. Armand's bedroom was considered the poorest one, being set just beneath the eaves on the side of the house that never caught the sun, but he liked it, because his was the only window that faced in the direction overlooking the wilder part of the hill, which was thick with thorn-bushes. It also had a fine view of the tips of the Devil's Claws, which really did look like claws from that angle.

The only other edifice that overlooked the same ground as Armand's attic was a tower-house situated on a further hillock, nested in a clump of dark trees and adjacent to a high-hedged garden. In the days of his early boyhood, Armand convinced himself that there was a mystery about that lonely house—and, more especially, about its garden, whose hedges were so high as to exclude the sun's direct rays entirely, save for a brief period around the hour of noon during the summer months. Many such impressions are lost as boys grow into youths, but Armand clung to his, and made a particular fetish out of that one.

While the adolescent Armand studied his books and practiced his script and figures, therefore, he would often sit by the window of his room, looking up occasionally to stare at the mysterious hedge. He knew that any flowers that grew in the garden must be exotic, not only because their beds were lighted for such a short time each day, but also because the thick and carefully-tailored hedge was so obviously designed to keep prying eyes at bay. Once or twice, when they had been children, he and Philippe had run the gauntlet of the intervening thorn-scrub to reach the bounds of the garden—for there was no path between the two houses—but they had never been able to find the slightest gap that might allow them to catch a glimpse of whatever lay within.

What Armand had been able to observe, however, and which had gradually acquired a sinister significance as he had grown older, was a certain strange traffic between the garden and the crags and marshes where the birds of Fourquevaux made their nests.

Most of the town's patient horticulturalists considered birds their enemies, for birds would sometimes come to dig up newly-embedded seeds, to spoil the flower-beds with their droppings as they flew overhead, or to devour the sweet produce of fruit-bearing bushes. In consequence, the horticulturalists usually employed bird-scarers, whose raucous hoots often combined in bizarre chorus. The gardener of the tower-house had no bird-scarer, though, and his garden was always silent, even when flocks of birds descended into it, as they sometimes did—especially in the early morning and the evening dusk, when the garden was entirely shadowed from the hesitant sun. As the hours that Armand spent watching the hedge from his bedroom window gradually increased, he became more and more convinced that many more birds flew down into the garden than ever flew up again.

Armand called the attention of Philippe Lekain to this phenomenon on more than one occasion, but Philippe assumed that his friend was trying to make a mystery out of nothing, and dismissed the assertion as both unlikely and irrelevant. This disinterest served only to make Armand more determined to find a mystery, and he began to search the pages in his books for records of carnivorous plants that were capable of trapping birds. He found various travelers' tales containing believable accounts of plants that trapped insects, and unbelievable accounts of plants that devoured men, but no trace of any rumor about plants whose preferred food was birds.

There was no road leading to the gate of the isolated tower-house, and the path that connected the gate to the main road connecting Fourquevaux to Is was narrow and winding, quite unsuited to dog-carts, let alone horse-drawn carriages. When Armand was not busy with his studies, he sometimes took it into his head to linger at the bottom of that path, waiting to catch a glimpse of the owner of the house—whose name, his father had gruffly informed him, was Gaspard Grouiller. When Armand had asked further questions his father had sternly disclaimed any further knowledge, and had stated that honest men did not pry into their neighbors' affairs.

Armand eventually ascertained, by careful collation of his occasional observations, that Grouiller only emerged from his solitary lair twice a week, on foot, carrying two large sacks, which he took to the marketplace and filled up with food. He began to make a careful study of the man, albeit from a distance, and followed him into the town on several occasions in order to watch him go about this humdrum business. Grouiller was tall and bald, with eyes that were very dark in color, but seemed unnaturally keen and bright. If he ever noticed that he was under observation by Armand he gave no sign of it.

Armand eventually ventured to ask several of the tradesmen who dealt with Grouiller what they knew of him, but none of them could tell what manner of man he was, or how he had earned the coin that he spent at their stalls. Not one of the tradesmen had an unfavorable word to say about his customer, however, and all of Armand's informants took scrupulous care to mention that their client always paid his debts.

On the other hand, Armand once saw a gypsy woman make a sign as Grouiller passed her by: a sign that was supposed to ward off the evil eye. That might have meant nothing at all, for gypsy women are notorious even today for being so anxious to ward off spells that they frequently make such signs without any reason or provocation, but Armand was nevertheless encouraged to believe that she might have a reason. He knew that gypsies were widely reputed to be clandestine followers of the Old Faith, and wondered whether Gaspard Grouiller might be known to the surviving Druids as a bad man.

On two or three occasions, when he knew that Grouiller was busy in the market, Armand took the opportunity to approach the façade of the lonely house and peer through its windows. He tried to peer through the hedge, too, as he had done when he was a boy, but it was still very thick as well as far too tall, and he could see no more now than he ever had. He could *hear* something from the other side, though—and what he heard was a low rustling sound, which might have been the sound of birds fluttering their wings as they moved among the branches of bushes, or even the murmur of their voices as they clucked and chattered to one another. These sounds fed his curiosity so teasingly that he hungered to find out more.

That hunger grew in him by degrees, until Armand became utterly determined that he would one day find a way to look into that garden, in order to find out what went on there in the shady hours of the early morning and the late afternoon. It was quite typical of his general frame of mind, though, that he never once considered taking a straightforward course, seeking to make the acquaintance of Gaspard Grouiller so that he might quite legitimately ask what plants the garden contained.

Armand knew that he had to get higher up if he was to see over the hedge of the enigmatic garden, and it seemed to him that there was only one way to contrive that feat. There was no other room above his, but the Kardan house had a steeply-sloped roof of red tile, and a chimney-stack, which would offer him an extra twelve or thirteen feet of elevation if only he could scale it.

Because this seemed a rather hazardous project, Armand called upon the help of his friend Philippe, asking the latter to secure a rope within his room and pay it out yard by yard while he climbed, in order that, if he were somehow to fall, the rope would save him from serious injury. Philippe agreed, albeit reluctantly, and waited impatiently when Armand had clambered out, wondering what possible account he could give to the Kardan family should the escapade go wrong.

Philippe need not have worried, because Armand soon came back through the window unharmed, in a state of high excitement.

"What did you see?" asked Philippe, caught up for once in the tangled threads of the mystery.

"I couldn't see very much," replied Armand, "but I saw a little more than I have seen before. There is a series of trellises—perhaps half a dozen, set in parallel at right-angles to the rear wall of the house. The trellis-work looks like the sort that is sometimes placed against the wall of a building to assist climbing roses and honeysuckle, but these structures are all free-standing. I could only see the tops of the trellises, but I was able to ascertain that they support flowers of several different hues—large flowers, with heads like trumpets. There are birds perching on the trellises, moving back and forth."

"And did you see any of these flowers seize and devour an unfortunate bird?" asked Philippe.

"No, I didn't," admitted Armand. "I haven't seen flowers of that kind before, though, and I'm sure that there's something strange about them."

"Oh, Armand!" said his friend sadly. "There are a hundred fine gardens in Fourquevaux, every one of which contains flowers whose proud owners cultivate them because they are unique. You now know the solution to the mystery of the high, dense hedge: it is to prevent squalls of wind from blowing down the free-standing trellises. What you have seen is, by your own account, quite ordinary; there is no reason whatsoever to suppose that what still remains hidden from you must be something strange and sinister."

"The birds are ordinary," Armand, admitted, "but I cannot help wondering whether the trellises might have been designed to provide perches for them as well as climbing-frames for the flower-bearing stems. I have never seen such flowers before, nor have I seen the kind of structure one which they are mounted. There is something odd about Gaspard Grouiller's garden."

"You have said yourself that the garden gets too little sun," Philippe insisted. "If the hedge has to be uncommonly tall to protect the garden from the winds to which the house is unusually exposed, the structures might also require to be uncommonly tall, not only to increase their ration of sunlight but in order to display the flowers to their proud cultivator."

If this speech had been intended to set Armand's mind at rest, it failed miserably. Armand was no longer listening to his friend; instead, he was standing by his window looking out in the direction of Gaspard Grouiller's house.

Philippe went to stand beside his friend, in order to see what he was looking at, and observed that the shutters of the only window in the third story of the tower-house that faced the Kardan house—which had been closed only a few minutes before, as they usually were—had now been thrown back. There was a man standing at the window, just as Armand was standing at his, and he was staring at the Kardan house, just as Armand was staring at the tower-house.

Philippe drew aside reflexively, but he could not resist peeping around the angle of the window, to see what would happen next.

After standing there for little more than a minute, Grouiller went away, leaving the shutters wide open.

"He must have seen you on the roof!" Philippe exclaimed.

"I suppose he must," Armand replied. "But what of it? A man may climb upon the roof of his own father's house, if he wants to!" Despite the bravado of his words, however, Armand's face was pale with anxiety, as if his blithe excitement had been turned by Grouiller's cool stare into incipient terror. "And yet," he muttered, hardly loud enough for Philippe to be able to hear the words, "there is some secret about that garden, and I'd dearly love to know what it is. I feel drawn to it, as if it had somehow put a spell on me."

"It's only a garden," Philippe reminded him, soothingly. "It's by no means the only one in Fourquevaux whose owner is jealous of his special blooms, or secretive about their quality."

That night, Armand closed the shutters of his window tightly, as he always did—as everyone tends to do in Bretagne, where the wind blowing from the ocean can carry a dire chill at night. When he fell asleep, though, he had a very curious dream.

He dreamt that there was a muffled sound, as if someone or something were tapping gently upon the shutters, combined with a fluttering sound, as if of wings in hectic motion, and followed by a sharp scraping sound, as if the talons of a claw were being dragged briefly across the outer face of each shutter.

Had he been awake, Armand might have clapped his hands to his ears and prayed for the morning to come, for he had heard all the usual children's tales about the various kinds of monsters that were reputed to haunt the Breton night—but he was not awake, and in his dream he rose from his bed to go to the window, and threw back the shutters, in order to look out boldly into the starlit night, as he had never dared to do before.

He was startled by the eerie brightness of the light that the stars gave, and as he peered into that imperfect gloom he saw black shadows moving within it: sinister night-flyers, larger by far than the birds that filled the sky by day.

Although he could not follow the trajectories of the shadows as they wheeled and soared in the starry sky. Armand became convinced that it was around the roof of the tower-house that they had gathered—and when he looked at the tower-house, he saw that the window from which Gaspard Grouiller had looked out that day was still unshuttered.

There was a red light burning within the room, and someone was standing by the window looking out, just as Armand was—perhaps Gaspard Grouiller, or perhaps someone else.

There was also a strange scent in the air—some exotic perfume—which intoxicated the dreamer as he breathed it in, and almost convinced him that he too could fly...but when he leaned a little further out of the bedroom widow, the dream began to fade away, and was lost.

The following day, when Armand tried to recall this dream, he could remember it quite clearly up to the point at which he had leaned out of the window, and could even remember it fading away—but he also had a curious impression that it had continued somehow, even though he was unconscious of its events. It was almost as if he had gone to sleep within his dream, and had then been delivered into a somnambulistic state, in which he had continued to act without being conscious of what he was doing.

Armand told this entire story to Philippe Lekain, and found himself quite carried away as he related it, so that he began to argue very fervently that the night-flyers he had seen were too huge to be ordinary birds, and must in fact have been demons briefly liberated from Hell by the permission of the Lord.

"Well, what of it?" Philippe countered. "In our dreams, we are subject to all manner of nightmares and delusions. We meet far more demons there than we are ever likely to encounter in everyday life."

Armand did not take offence at this remark, but simply took his friend to the window, where the shutters had been thrown back to let in the daylight. He pulled one of them back until it was closed, and invited Philippe to crane his neck and inspect its outer surface. The he opened that one and pulled the other back in order to allow a similar inspection.

Philippe saw that there were three long scratches in the wood, extending across both shutters; when he measured their span with his hand, he shuddered to think what manner of claw it might have been that had made them.

"But after all," Philippe said, stubbornly, "even if the scratching sound *was* real, and some strange bird or bat really did harass your shutters, the rest was only a dream. You did not actually rise from your bed and open the shutters, did you?"

"Didn't I?" Armand said, quizzically. Then, after a moment's hesitation, he threw the shutters wide open again. "You're right," he said. "I didn't—and I surely never will, if anything similar happens again."

Armand attempted to put Gaspard Grouiller out of his thoughts for the remainder of that day, and returned with a new will to the study of a witchfinder's manual that had been sold to him by a colporteur, which had much to say about the vile practices and heretical beliefs of the fugitive adherents of the Old Faith. He tried not to let his mind dwell on the matter of the mysterious garden, but could not help pausing whenever he found a reference to the plants that had made up the Druidic herbarium, lest he find some clue regarding the nature of the unknown blooms that he had seen upon the trellis in the hidden garden. There were far too many plants briefly mentioned in connection with the worship of the Old Faith, however, with far too little in the way of description to allow them to be easily identified. The patient monk who had compiled the manual had been primarily interested in other matters.

On the next night, and the next after that, Armand slept very fitfully. Once or twice he was convinced that he heard the nearby flutter of wings, but nothing tapped at his shutters and nothing scratched the wood. He did not dream—indeed, it seemed to him that whenever he was about to escape from anxious wakefulness into the comfort of a dream he was rudely snatched back from its brink by his own lurking anxieties, in order that he might continue to toss and turn upon his pallet.

By day, Armand tried to tell himself that he had now done everything reasonably possible to fathom the mystery, and must be content to let it alone. Indeed, he almost contrived to convince himself that he had quite had enough of Gaspard Grouiller's garden, and did not care about it any more—but this private assertion was a mere sham, which could not stand the test of temptation.

* * * * * * *

Three days after his expedition on to the roof of his father's house, Armand and Philippe were walking in the street on market day, intent on their conversation, when they suddenly found their way blocked. When they looked up to see who had accosted them, they were most surprised to discover that it was Gaspard Grouiller.

"You're Kardan's son, are you not?" the bald man said, addressing Armand, after directing a brief but polite smile at Philippe. "You're my nearest neighbor, I believe. You seem to be very interested in my garden."

All the color had drained from Armand's cheeks, and he was too tongue-tied to make any reply.

"I'd love to show it off to you, now that the proper season has arrived," Grouiller continued, amiably. "The birds like to visit it, as you must have observed, but I receive very few human visitors. Fourquevaux is a town where people like to keep themselves to themselves, and it's not an easy place in which to make friends."

Armand still did not seem disposed to reply, so Philippe hastened to intervene, saying, only a little uncertainly: "You're very kind, sir. Armand and I would be very glad to admire your flowers. You're quite right, alas, about the difficult of making friends in Fourquevaux. I think it's because so many outsiders settle here; it doesn't have the same elaborate network of family relationships as its neighboring villages."

Grouiller responded to these polite observations with an oddly formal bow. "The time isn't exactly right just yet," he said. "I'd like you to see the blooms at their very best—which will hopefully be in slightly less than a week's time. If we're fortunate, they'll likely be in full bloom on Monday next, if you'd like to call round then."

"Would noon be convenient?" Philippe asked.

"Quite convenient," the generous horticulturalist replied, bowing again before he walked on.

"Well," said Philippe, proudly, to his silent friend, "here's a chance to set your mind at rest for once and for all. We'll see his garden at its finest, and the mystery will be over and done with. I do think you might have spoken to him yourself, though. He seems a pleasant enough fellow, after all, and he's right about the tendency of the townspeople to keep themselves to themselves, even to the point of neglecting common formulas of hospitality."

Armand opened his mouth, as if to disagree or complain, but in the end he simply nodded his head. "Perhaps it's for the best," he said. "We'll go together, and see what there is to be seen."

Armand told his father about this invitation, and asked again what the elder Kardan knew about his neighbor, but the tradesman simply shrugged his shoulders and said that people had no right to pry into the affairs of their neighbors unless their credit was suspect—and that, so far as he knew, Gaspard Grouiller had no significant debts.

At the appointed hour, therefore, Philippe and Armand made their way up the path to Grouiller's door. When Armand knocked, the signal was promptly answered, and their host welcomed them into his house. The ground-floor rooms were rather dingy, and somewhat cramped by virtue of the excessive number of chairs they contained, but they did not seem in any way unusual. The quality of the rugs and wall-hangings suggested that Grouiller was not a poor man, but they were all rather old and somewhat faded. There was no obvious indication there of the owner's former occupation. They did not linger long inside the house, however, before Grouiller ushered his guests out of the side door that served as the entrance to the garden.

As they came through the garden door, the sight that met their eyes caused Philippe to draw in his breath quite sharply, and Armand released a gasp of surprise that was almost a tiny scream.

As Armand had already discovered, the middle of the garden was occupied by a series of parallel structures, which he had mistakenly taken for trellis-work. At close range, however, it was obvious that the structures were actually living plants: trees or bushes which, instead of growing radially from a rounded central trunk to form a conventional dendrite, grew from a flattened trunk in the two dimensions of a plane. Each of the structures—there were six in all—was composed of a single dendrite whose plate-like trunk divided into two main branches, each of which followed a sinuous path as the two branches meandered away in exactly opposite directions, so that their densely-aggregated sub-branches filled in all the available space in the upward and lengthwise directions, while refusing to exploit the dimension of breadth at all, save for the minimal necessity of physical presence. Its was as if each of the six plants was determined to form a natural fence or wall, exactly parallel to those formed by its neighbors.

The distances between the six living fences seemed to have been measured out with uncanny exactitude, all five gaps being exactly similar, amply wide enough to permit a man to walk between them comfortably. The gaps to either side of the outermost dendrites, separating them from the hedges, were considerably larger, but still seemed reminiscent of tunnels simply because the structures and the hedge were so high. Although the summits of each wall-like dendrite were exposed to the sunlight, the lower branches were deeply shadowed.

The path that led from the doorway of the house extended into the corridor between the dendrite on the extreme left and the hedge, then looped back into the first alley, and then the next, making a sequence of five hairpin turns before returning to complete its loop without traversing the interval between the dendrite on the far right and the hedge on that side. Before guiding them along this path, however, Gaspard Grouiller paused to allow his guests to study the entire aggregation, as it were, end-on.

Five narrow lanes extended before Armand and Philippe, although the only one whose far end they could presently see was the first. Their immediate impulse was to look up, to the ridges as the tops of the trees, where the horizontally-set branches offered convenient perches for birds of various sorts—and in which dozens of birds were, indeed, contentedly perched. There too, the flowers that boomed on the branches were exposed to the sun and fully open, displaying broad corollas of various hue, ranging from imperial purple through sky-blue and orange to blood-red. The perching birds did not seem to be paying any attention at all to the flowers, seemingly unattracted by any perfume they might be emitting and quite unintimidated by their brightness.

Then, however, the eyes of the two adolescents were drawn downwards, into the shadowed intervals between the foliage-sheets of the two-dimensional trees. There were flowers growing there too; indeed, all the branches seemed to be putting forth flowers, including the lowest of all, which were lying horizontally upon the bare ground. The flowers just beneath those at the top, however, had much more subtle colors, and those which grew lower still, in the gloomier regions of the arbor, had no color at all; their petals were pure white, and the sexual parts of each flower—the central style and its surrounding circle of rigid stamens—were jet black.

There were birds lower down, too, but they were not perching, and they were far from content. The walls formed by the complex network of branches were evidently equipped with some kind of invisible adhesive, like transparent birdlime, whose effect commenced an inch or two beneath the branches forming the ridge. Unwary perching individuals obviously became stuck on occasion, but were presumably unable to react to their capture by struggling or emitting warning cries.

Perhaps, Armand thought, the adhesive was also a powerful narcotic; at any rate, birds that did become stuck obviously accepted their fate meekly. They did not remain where they were, however; as well as the capture-mechanisms, the strange branches were also equipped with some means of moving their prey in a downward direction, gradually passing the feathered bodies from one branch to another.

As the avian corpses made this descent, their plumage gradually lost its color, in much the same fashion as the flowers among which they passed—but they also lost their shape and mass in the same degree, as their flesh was slowly absorbed into that of the plant. The shriveling bodies vanished completely, it seemed, before they reached ground-level.

Although the movement of the corpses was too slow to be measured by the naked eye, there were so many bodies within each alleyway, at various different heights, ranging in distinctness in strict proportion to their position from easily-identifiable but utterly quiet birds to mere undifferentiated bulges, that it was perfectly obvious to Armand and Philippe what kind of process was confronting them.

Gaspard Grouiller said nothing for several minutes, being quite content to study his guests' faces and smile at their confusion. Eventually, though, he said: "I know that you have never seen anything like this before, my young friends. There's nothing like this in any other garden in Fourquevaux—or, I dare hope, in all Bretagne. The walltree's native habitat is in another continent, which can only be reached by ocean-going ships, and whose very existence is secret to all but a few very dedicated mariners loyal to Prince Gradlon, the greatest of all the merchant-monarchs of Is."

He led the two youths along the path that ran alongside the outer surface of the dendrite on the extreme left, pointing out the place where the flat trunk was embedded in the soil.

"Its roots grow in exactly the same two-dimensional pattern," the enthusiastic horticulturalist told his guests. "It is a highly advanced adaptation, for it puts an end to the vulgar competition for three dimensional space in which primitive trees are permanently involved; walltrees are the plant kingdom's equivalent of civilized men, ordering their affairs by careful agreement—which they can afford to do, for they are also as omnivorous as civilized men, obtaining much of their nourishment from meat, as do the human elite.

There were more colored flowers on the outside of the endmost "walltree", because its upper branches had slightly more exposure to the sun. but there were fewer captive birds embedded in its outer surface than its inner one—a fact that became increasingly obvious as the path turned back on itself and Armand and Philippe followed Gaspard Grouiller into the heart of his determinedly undeceptive maze.

It was very dark indeed in the interior corridors of the exotic copse, and surprisingly cold. Although there was space enough for the three men to walk in single file, with plenty of elbow-room, Armand could not help feeling horribly hemmed in. The white flowers that grew at and below head-heights seemed quite phantasmal, and the black stigmas projecting from their cores put him uncomfortable in mind of avid tongues. Even so, the flowers were less discomfiting than the bulges fading into shapeless, which had once been living birds.

Armand kept his arm tightly stuck to his sides, terrified to reach out in case he touched the seemingly-fragile wall of vegetation and became stick to it himself, thus beginning a process of patient absorption—to which he would be unable to put up any resistance, because he would be anaesthetized into equally patient acceptance of his fate.

The birds perching high above his head, or fluttering about the margins of the extraordinary garden, were chirping in a seemingly cheerful fashion, but as the sound of their calls descended into the cavernous depths of the walltree array it seemed to strike strange echoes, which transformed the chorus into a kind of lament, if not an actual dirge.

As Armand had observed from the roof of his house, the birds were all perfectly ordinary. They included gulls from the Devil's Claws, waders from the marshes and passerines from the great forest of Leonais, all happily mingling together just as mariners from many lands mingled in the narrow streets huddled about the harbor of Is.

The birds gathered on the narrow summit of each wall-tree were not all still. Some were hopping aimlessly about, as if they too were visitors invited there to enjoy the beauty of the blooms; they went about their promenades quite unmolested. Armand judged that it was not until they settled down that they were in danger of finding themselves incapable of take off again, and perhaps incapable of wanting to; only then could they be gently seized and slowly pulled downwards, without ever having uttered a cry of alarm.

As he moved back and forth within the structure, Armand tried not to think about the birds—which had, after all, ceased to bear any particular resemblance to birds by the time their residues reached head-height—but he found it only a little less disconcerting to focus his attention on the flowers. The largest of them were about the size of a man's head, and their black stigmas were as long as his thumb, although they were more rounded, and rather bulbous at the tip.

"Those flowers are exceptionally fine," Gaspard Grouiller assured his guests. "In their wild state, they do not grow nearly so large, nor are they so fecund in their production of nectar."

"Nectar?" Philippe queried. "The white flowers have a strange odor, to be sure, but it does not have the sweetness of nectar. I cannot imagine, in any case, that they are pollinated by bees. Why, given that circumstance, would they produce nectar?"

"I see that you are something of a horticulturalist yourself, Master Lekain," said Grouiller. "You understand the magical symbiosis that links flowering plants to their animal pollinators. You are quite right to observe that the walltree's flowers are not pollinated by bees, and that the odor of their nectar is by no means sweet, at least by day. You will also notice, however, that the white flowers—unlike their colored cousins up above—open in the gloom, and they remain open even in the depths of the darkest nights. It is then that their pollinators visit them, and the black nectar is consumed. It is considered quite a delicacy by some, I believe, but it's not entirely to my taste. I dare say that I could sell it for a good price in Is were I to take the trouble to bottle it, but I retired some while ago from that kind of commerce."

"*Black* nectar?" Philippe queried. "What kind of pollinators does it attract in the dead of night? Moths? Or bats perhaps?"

"Perhaps," said Gaspard Grouiller, as he came to the end of the tightly-wound pathway and stepped back into the daylight near the door to his house. "I must confess that I am not entirely sure. I sleep by night, as other men do, with my shutters tightly closed. Well, Master Kardan, how do you like my garden? Has it lived up to your expectations? Is it not extraordinarily beautiful?"

Armand did not know how to reply, at first, but he eventually found his tongue. "They *are* very beautiful," he admitted. He was still standing in the mouth of the alleyway, and he had only to make a quarter-turn in order to reach up as if to touch one of the flowers, but he only moved his finger round in mid-air, without actually touching the rim of the corolla or the tip of the stigma.

Grouiller smiled, and stepped back in order to stand beside Armand, while Philippe moved out of the way. The horticulturalist reached up to the same flower, and applied the tip of his forefinger very gently to the tip of the stigma. When he took the finger away he showed Armand the tiny droplet of black liquid that the stigma had exuded.

"Don't worry," Grouiller said. "Black nectar is by no means poisonous." He put his finger into his mouth then, and licked the droplet away. As he did so, his sleeve fell away from his unusually thin forearm, and Armand was surprised to see that the form of his hand was slightly deformed, and that the fingers were somewhat reminiscent the claws of a bird.

"You may try it if you wish," the horticulturalist said. "It will do you no harm—and, as I said, some people rather like it."

Armand hesitated, but then he touched his own index finger to the same stigma, which emitted a tiny black droplet. Armand put out his tongue, very gingerly, and touched the droplet to its tip.

"Why, yes," he said, making no attempt to conceal his surprise. "It's certainly strange, but not unpleasant."

Grouiller and Armand both looked at Philippe then, tacitly inviting him to try the experiment for himself—but Philippe looked away, and pretended not to notice. Armand followed his gaze, and noticed for the first time that the gap between the last walltree and the hedge was not empty, as the one they had initially traversed had been.

There were five giant toadstools growing in the passage, arranged in an approximate W-formation, with the middle point of the set of three noticeably closer to the walltrees than its two companions. Each one had a thick chitinous pedestal and a wide black cap speckled with silver, as if it were mirroring a starry night.

This pattern was so odd that Armand thought briefly they might be carved from stone—but when he took a step closer he saw that they had the authentic texture of fungal flesh. He was a little reluctant to touch one merely to make sure of that, but Gaspard Grouiller was still looking at him in a challenging fashion, so he went to set his hand upon the nearest cap.

"It's warm!" he said, in surprise.

"They're ugly things, by comparison with my beautiful wall-trees," Grouiller said, with an apologetic sigh, "but not everything rare is precious, and these are no more common than my lovely blossoms. They are not so attractive to birds or humans, but they have their own place in the scheme of Nature, as all things have."

This little speech reminded Armand of his earlier conviction that Grouiller was known to the followers of the Old Faith, and he wondered if the man might be a Druid, who cultivated these strange things because of some virtue that they had. It was not the sort of matter that could be raised in polite conversation, though, so he held his tongue.

As Grouiller led his guests back to the house he said to Philippe: "Perhaps you think it slightly cruel to cultivate plants that feed on birds—but they *are* very beautiful flowers, are they not? And Fourquevaux has no shortage of birds, as you must certainly agree. There is room in the wide world for many different kinds of gardens, and many different kinds of beauty."

Afterwards, the horticulturist stood outside his front door, watching the two youths as they walked down the path towards the town—but he had gone back inside by the time they turned the corner that took them out of sight.

* * * * * * *

Philippe was eager to discuss what they had seen in Gaspard Grouiller's garden with his friend, but he found Armand oddly disinclined to accommodate him. It had surprised Philippe to learn that Armand's wild surmise about the fate of the birds that visited the garden was actually correct, and it seemed to him an item of gossip worth spreading—for Grouiller had not asked them to keep silent about what they had seen. Armand, on the other hand, seemed only to desire solitude and the company of his books, so Philippe soon left him alone.

When night fell, Armand closed and locked the shutters of his window as usual, and went to his bed in a state of some exhaustion, having slept so badly of late. This time, however, sleep came very quickly to claim him, and he did not toss and turn at all. He was later to tell Philippe that he believed he had slept dreamlessly for a long while before he was visited by a very dreadful nightmare.

The nightmare began, as had his peculiar dream of some days earlier, with the sound of something attempting to gain admission at his window—first by rapping, as if to demand that he open the shutters, and then by tearing at the edge of the wood with clawed fingers. In the end, Armand subsequently explained to his friend, his dream-self had risen from the bed and gone to the window, unlocking the shutters and throwing them open.

There, hanging upside-down from the eaves like a great bat was a monstrous creature with brightly-colored feathered wings and a manlike face with thick, rubbery lips. Its body resembled a plucked bird, the skin all puckered and dappled, and its limbs (of which there were four in addition to the wings) were like the limbs of eagles, scaly and taloned.

This creature snatched at Armand's dream-self, and lifted him as though he weighed hardly anything at all—but this action was not hostile, and almost seemed protective, for, as the demon launched itself into flight, it hugged Armand to its bosom as a mother might clutch a child. Fearful of falling, Armand wrapped his arms about the waist of the peculiar creature, as if accepting and returning its embrace. He reported to Philippe that, as they flew through the air, he could feel the beating of the great muscles in the demon's breast, where his face was pressed against the wrinkled skin. There were, he said, no teats upon that breast at which an infant might suck.

The flight was a short one, which only took him to the hillock on which Gaspard Grouiller's house stood. The second-story window facing the Kardan house was wide open and brightly-lit, as if the tower were a lighthouse for insidious winged monsters, which haunted Fourquevaux at night. Armand was delivered by his carrier into the garden beside the house, and found himself in the space between the end of the bower and the five great toadstools, whose formation no longer resembled a ragged W, as Armand now perceived it, but an elongated pentagram.

Inside the pentagram stood a creature like the one that had brought him, but bigger by far, standing almost as tall as that strange high hedge. Its vast wings were feathered like those of the legendary firebird, glowing silver and gold from within. Its capacious arms were stretched aloft, with the claws widespread as though to catch the silver light of the bountiful stars. Its slender legs had flattened feet like those of a fowl, so that it could stand upon the ground instead of searching for a perch, as its smaller companions had to do.

The expression on the monster's face, as it looked at Armand, was horridly paradoxical. The face—so Armand told Philippe—was uglier than he could ever have imagined, with horrid bloodshot eyes and a nose like a huge serrated beak, mounted above a mouth crowded with sharpened teeth, and yet, Armand said, the gaze of those foul eyes was not predatory at all, but exceedingly fond, and the black tongue that crawled in serpentine fashion between the cluttered teeth was not licking the outer lips as if in anticipation of a meal, but teasing him with its little motions as a mother might tease her child with friendly grimaces.

When his dream-self had borne this inspection for a few long minutes, Armand felt himself taken up again, and lifted up to the series of parallel ridges, where the brightest and the best flowers grew—and he was tenderly placed among them, in the middle of a crowd of perching demons.

Armand already knew what to do, and bowed his head immediately to a succulent bloom, taking the central style into his mouth as all the others were doing, sucking greedily at the jet-black milk contained within, carefully prepared by the wondrous flowers from the tender flesh of captured birds.

The taste of that nectar, Armand said, was not at all sweet, and strangely unappetizing—but it was only an appetizer. After a few moments, the demons began to descend into the intervals within the array of walltrees, and Armand crept down with them, finding no difficulty at all in maintaining his adhesion to the surfaces of the walltrees, but never becoming stuck.

He drank at flower after flower, and immediately discerned the different flavors that the black nectar presented as he descended into the depths of the undeceptive maze—which now seemed bottomless, as if its corridors cut deep into the heart of the world, perhaps extending all the way to Hell.

The whitest flowers, which produced the blackest and best nectar of all, seemed even more phantasmal now than they had before.

Eventually, the dream faded away—and in the morning, when he woke up, Armand could remember that fading process. It was, he said, as if he were going to sleep within his dream.

* * * * * * *

When Armand related this dream to Philippe, he assured him that there must have been further events, which he could not remember by virtue of the quasi-somnambulistic state into which he had fallen within the dream, and that his wild adventures must have continued for several hours, even though he could not recall a single detail of them.

Philippe was considerably more impressed by this dream than he had been by the first one that Armand had related. He was almost ready to believe that there was something truly awful about the garden that they had seen, and that Gaspard Grouiller might actually have signed some dire pact with the demons of Fourquevaux—and yet, he told himself as he listened to Armand's feverish recital, a dream is only a dream, and the shutters at the window had never in fact been opened, nor were there any additional scratches to be seen upon their outer face.

With these doubts in mind, Philippe told Armand that his nightmare, however frightening it may have been, could not be taken seriously as a revelation. Perhaps, he suggested, the dream had been a kind of release, by which all the anxiety that Armand had been storing up had at last been discharged.

Armand dismissed this explanation out of hand. "There's more," he said, excitedly, "for when I woke this morning, and went to my books, I finally discovered a passage in the witchfinder's manual for which I've been searching for so long—the passage that helps to explain what manner of thing these monstrous flowers are, and what dreadful harm they can do."

So saying, Armand placed the open book before his friend—but Philippe could not read, and Armand was forced to read what was written there aloud.

"The followers of the Druid Faith," he quoted, "believe that every living element of the natural world is properly destined for the nourishment of others. As the flower feeds the bee, which will make honey for the bear, so the leaf feeds the worm, which will later take flight as a brightly colored thing, which will feed the perching bird, which feeds the hawk, which will fall in time to earth, as the bear falls also, to feed the tiny things that crowd the fertile soil, where the roots draw nourishment to feed the flower and the leaf. So it is that everything that lives is born from the soil and the sea and the air, and must return in time to soil and sea and air, so that all may be renewed, forever and ever without pause or end.

"This belief might be innocuous if it were to merely restricted to an ignorant account of the Lord's providence, but it is extended, as might be expected of a demonically-inspired credo, into objectionable forms. The Druid priests also contend that there is an evil in the world, which seeks to pervert the weave of destiny. That evil, they claim—and should surely know—is capable of altering the flower or the leaf to become the nourishment of *demons*, so as to spread the seed of malice within the world.

"Those who make this contention, in writings which the Church takes great care to destroy, lest the innocent be corrupted, pretend to be issuing warnings to the unwary, but that is deceptive, for they are demon-led themselves. Witchfinders must be wary of such trickery, and it is for that reason alone that these warnings may be conserved for the benefit of the Lord's most devoted soldiers. One such warning, which has particular relevance in Bretagne, and the evil city of Is, takes the following form:

"*Beware the treasonous beauty of blooms whose nectar is food for demons; they harbor the black milk of ecstasy, which promises destruction.*"

When he heard this, Philippe Lekain felt a chill in his heart, and for just one moment he saw the world as Armand Kardan had always seen it: as a peculiar and magical place, full of threats and confusions, in which no man could truly live in comfort and safety. It was not the kind of world in which he desired to spend the remainder of his days.

"Can you not see," said Armand, "that Gaspard Grouiller keeps his garden for the nourishment of demons, who fly there by night? I cannot tell whether he is their servant or their master, or what he may have to do with the other horrid things that happen in Fourquevaux by night, but this I know: that man's soul is no longer his own, and his garden is a thing so vile as to terrify the mind of any honest man!"

Philippe would have none of this, however. "Armand," he said, truly believing that he was reaching out a helping hand to save his friend from unnecessary and unworthy terrors, "this is mere nonsense. The Old Faith is the superstition of gypsies and the ragged men of the forests, and witchfinders take it too seriously when they condemn it as a threat to good Christians. We are civilized men, and we have Christ for our guide and guardian. The excellent horticulturalists of Fourquevaux have shown us that the flowers of the wild are there to be tamed, arranged and regimented to our pleasure. Gaspard Grouiller is only a gardener, after all—a common eccentric. He does not seek to make a secret of his garden, but willingly invited us into it to show off his pride in his achievement. Lay down that silly book, I beg you, and take up others, which will teach you the ways of the merchant in the marketplace and the arts of civilized men."

Armand looked long and hard at his friend, but said nothing, and finally laid the book down. They both went to the window, in order to stare at the distant tower-house and the tall dark hedge that surrounded its garden. "Did we really play in that thorny wilderness when we were children?" Philippe asked, with a small laugh. "The bushes must have been sparser then, for I am sure that we could not find a way among them now without being scratched half to death."

"It was a long time ago," Armand replied. "And we were little children then, very different from what we have now become."

* * * * * * *

Early the next day, Armand's mother came to his room to search for him, because he had not come to breakfast. She found the room empty, with the bed in disarray and the shutters wide open. She went to the window and looked out, and immediately saw her son's body, some little distance from the wall, deep in the bosom of a thorn-bush, covered in blood.

It was not easy to reach the body, and the elder Kardan had to call upon the assistance of his neighbors to hack a way through to it. Philippe was one of those who helped with this dire work, and was therefore able to see the corpse of his friend before it was taken—with great difficulty—from the bush.

It was obvious that Armand must have fallen into the bush from a considerable height. The only hypothesis that could be offered by way of rational explanation was that he had undone the shutters of his window during the hours of darkness, climbed up on to the roof of the house, and launched himself therefrom in a prodigious leap, which had delivered him inevitably to his fate.

The thorns had punctured him in very many places, hard-driven by the force of his fall, and when the would-be rescuers had finally pulled him free of the bush, they saw that there was hardly an inch of his flesh unmolested. It was almost as if he had been raked and rent by a multitude of angry claws.

When the company returned to the Kardan house Philippe told his companions about the nightmares that Armand had lately suffered, and about their visit to Gaspard Grouiller's strange garden. Because it was the first time he had told the story, it was somewhat confused in the telling—far more confused than the many versions he was to tell when he grew to full manhood, and then to old age—but it would probably have made no difference if every detail had been in its proper place, for his audience was comprised of urban tradesmen. Although such people they bolt their doors most carefully at night, they are ever inclined to believe that whatever the dark might hide is no concern of theirs.

Nightmares, these particular civilized men agreed, were a sign of madness and folly—and if any more proof were needed that poor Armand had been sadly deranged, one only had to look at the peculiar books he had chosen to buy and to read.

As for Gaspard Grouiller, the elder Kardan and all his friends were unanimous in declaring him a good enough neighbor. If the plants in his garden captured and devoured birds, that was certainly peculiar, but Fourquevaux had no shortage of birds, and the great majority of them were a nuisance to other gardeners, so Grouiller's activities had to be counted to the public good. If any further proof were needed that the horticulturalist was fully worthy to live among honest tradespeople, it was universally acknowledged that he was a man who always settled his debts promptly, and in full.

NEPHTHYS

In the dim and distant past there was a petty realm that lay far beyond the southern bounds of Arabia, in the lush hot lands beyond the great sand sea, which was ruled for a while by a queen named Nephthys. Her reign was soon forgotten, for her people never learned the art of writing and preserved no history, but it was remarkable in its fashion, at least in its final years.

In the days of her youth Nephthys was reasonably contented, and let her subjects alone, but when she became restless upon her ivory throne, she turned to persecution as a form of amusement. Like all other forms of amusement, however, oppression became tedious, and there came a time when all its resources seemed exhausted. Nephthys then fell prey to a terrible *ennui*. The ingenious execution of a faithless lover served to lift the burden of her sorrow very briefly, but it was a sour pleasure, made all the sourer by the knowledge that there was none very eager to take his place. Age had begun to cast its blight upon her face.

The heart of Nephthys then became saturated with dreadful anxiety; she yearned desperately for some particular shock that might quicken the blood in her veins again, but there remained no euphoric cup that she had not already drained to the uttermost dreg, and no delicious immorality that she had hoarded for this drear time. Weariness worked in her soul like a canker, and in her mind's eye she saw her future, mapped out for her by the slow and subtle corruption that had already robbed her of her youth, her beauty and her pride.

In consequence of this revelation she summoned her two most accomplished wizards, and commanded them to abandon their allegiance to the petty and parsimonious demons that they had served until then. She instructed them to offer their prayers instead to some darker and more fervent godling, in order that, with its aid, she might strive to break the chain of ice that clutched at her soul, and light again the dying embers of her lost vitality.

One of the wizards refused to contemplate such a terrible heresy, and Nephthys instructed her guards to slay him on the spot. This was done, at the cost of a few trivial magical penalties. The second wizard, whose name was Ghazafar, immediately realized the necessity of consigning his soul to the care of a more powerful protector, for his own sake as well as his queen's.

Ghazafar made what shift he could to acquaint themselves with demons whose horrible like he had never cared to know before, and contrived in the end to attract the attention of a mighty prince of the demonic kind, who condescended to be conjured by men by means of the name of Xhoris Alaquel. After much effort, he succeeded in inflicting possession by this prince of demons upon a young slave.

"I am Xhoris Alaquel, Lord of Change," said the demon to his summoner, in a distant and condescending manner, "and there is such sorcery in my sight that all of ambition and anxiety are open to my gaze. What a man has done and what he has become are not the best of him, nor yet the worst, for there echoes in the coverts of his soul the things he might have been but only dreamed or feared to be....and in those yearning echoes, the seeds of my worship are."

"Forgive me, Lord," said Ghazafar to the possessive demon, "for drawing your attention to such a petty kingdom as this, which hath but a few paltry souls within its bounds, many of which are deeply steeped in that virtue which so often attaches itself to abject poverty. You, who see so much more deeply into the souls of men than a pitiful charlatan like myself, will know far better than I what challenges and prizes it has to offer. I think I may say without fear or favor, however, that its queen is as deliciously wicked a monarch as has ever walked upon the earth, and might make a useful instrument for one such as yourself, if only her health and beauty might be fully replenished."

"I am Xhoris Alaquel, Lord of Change," the demon continued, seemingly oblivious to matters of mere detail, "and there is such warmth and bewitchment in my temptations that none shall have the strength to resist me, save only those unfortunates who have no flames of unsatisfied desire burning in their souls."

"There are not many of those in the kingdom," Ghazafar agreed, reflectively, "and the desires of the queen of which I spoke burn exceeding hot. But you will doubtless decide for yourself whether it is worth your while to dally here for a while."

"I am here," replied Xhoris Alaquel, and left it at that.

For Nephthys' sake, Ghazafar made the dire pledges required to bind Xhoris Alaquel to the earth for a time; and for the sake of Xhoris Alaquel, he summoned Nephthys so that she might make a bloody pact to be redeemed by the souls of her subjects.

"What can you promise me," asked Nephthys of the demon, "if I make you a gift of my realm and all my subjects, and my own rich royal blood?"

"I am Xhoris Alaquel, Lord of Change," answered the demon, "and there is such wrath and tenderness about my touch that nothing can resist my fond caress. So come to me, my anguished and melancholy child, and I will show you splendor, and soothe away your shame. We will make a pageant of the traffic of the world and a carnival of its destruction."

"Be more specific," she demanded sharply, so haughty in her majesty that she dared speak thus even to a prince of demons.

"I can promise you beauty more magnificent and sensations more fierce than any you have ever known," said the possessive demon, seemingly careless of her audacity—although his host's captive eyes glittered strangely as he added, "and wisdom more arcane, of course."

"I leave wisdom to my underlings," Nephthys replied, glancing sideways at Ghazafar, who was frowning with anxiety.

"You should not," said the demon, tranquilly. "It is the most delicate and most piquant of all the pleasures. To know the secrets of the souls of men, in life and in eternity, is the most delicious sensation of all."

"In that case," said Nephthys, "I desire it. Give me marvelous beauty, fabulous sensation, and spicy wisdom, and I will make my kingdom a veritable riot of cruel torments and orgiastic indulgencies, in honor of the name of Xhoris Alaquel."

Despite that it was such a petty price, Xhoris Alaquel did as he was bid. He made the queen more beautiful than she had been in the most glorious days of her youth, taught her the secrets of the most exotic drugs, sharpened her responses to the myriad extremes of erotic sensation, and instructed her as to the innermost secrets of the human soul. He transformed his temporary host in like manner, so that he might become her consort in every desirable way, and he employed the quiet times after their love-making for her philosophical education.

"A man is but a storehouse of frustrated fantasies and formications," he explained to her, "whose empty spaces are haunted by terrors, which—he knows!—he can never quite escape. No man wins free from hope or horror until he is committed to the grave, *and some do not have leave to be settled and still even then....*"

And again:

"A man is but a rattling bag of bones, stirred by restless passions that he cannot properly control, or even understand, so that he hates the best and worst of his impulses alike, and hates his remorse even more. And yet, were Change begone from his being....were there no more daemonic fury to stir and sully him....what would he be but a bag of lumpen bones, heavy with the burden of oblivion?"

And again:

"Men were not made for eternal sleep, but for dreaming; and so it is that dreaming alone can drive a man awake through the grey and wintry days and the black uncaring nights. Without the dreams that drive him, a man is but a thing of sodden, sullen earth, a quaking hull of that rough-hewn clay which is called flesh. Without the angry nightmares that disturb him, a man is but a blind thing, which cannot see the golden fire of life...a deaf thing, which cannot hear the beating of the Heart Divine...a mute thing, which cannot cry at all."

Nephthys saw, in good time, that all of this was true. All of her experience confirmed it: all the new sensations that she learned to enjoy; all the new cruelties that she was now delighted to inflict upon her subjects; all the original flights of fancy that carried her away.

The queen was faithful to her promises, and persisted in her oppressions with enthusiasm, increasing their violence tenfold. She used every means available to her to drive virtue from her realm. Where terror was ineffective she used seduction, and with Xhoris Alaquel to aid her she was irresistible. The wisdom with which he endowed her shaped and guided her power, and made her a force of corruption more corrosive than any the world had ever known. She presided over the promised riot of excess with pride and exuberance, taking all the more pleasure from the tortures she inflicted because she knew that they were merely a prelude to eternal damnation.

Nephthys loved all the kinds of love-making to which the demon introduced her, but the kind which she loved best was that which took place on the wing, for she loved to don the plumage of a bird and fly into the cloudless sky, high into the cheerless vault of heaven. Some of her new pleasures eventually began to pall, as earthly pleasures tend to do, but that one never did.

"When the time comes for me to deliver up my soul," she said to her demon lover—as if it were a command rather than a request— "I would be quit of it while I am soaring to a great heights, swooning for the rarity of the air."

"As you wish," he answered, politely—with the hint of a cynical gleam in his untender eye.

He was true to his word. The time came when her avian amorist carried Nephthys higher than ever before into the avid sky, where he raked her with his furious claws, and claimed the noblest of all the souls that had been promised to him. There was giddy laughter mingled with her screams of pain, for Nephthys knew well enough how burdensome her life must have become, as the pleasures of the flesh continued to pall. While Xhoris Alaquel tore her earthly body apart she thought of his ecstatic fury as a kind of salvation.

How wise I was to accept wisdom, she thought, *for wisdom will teach me to bear damnation far better than my ignorant subjects ever could.*

She was wrong, but not because Xhoris Alaquel had in any way betrayed her. She took her wisdom with her to the world beyond the grave, so that she might understand the innermost secrets of the human soul, and thus she was empowered to know *exactly* what it meant to be in Hell, without sleep, without dreams, without release.

In Hell, for the first time and for all eternity, she contrived to comprehend what she had not quite managed to comprehend before: that death need not end desire, in ending the possibility of its fulfillment. In Hell, for the first time and for all eternity, she discovered that a wisdom formed in words may have to be experienced before its true significance can be appreciated. In Hell, for the first time and for all eternity, she realized what the fatefully informative pronouncements of Xhoris Alaquel the teacher really meant.

"A man is but a storehouse of frustrated fantasies and formications," he had told her, with beguiling and deceptive honesty, "whose empty spaces are haunted by terrors, which—he knows!—he can never quite escape. No man wins free from hope or horror until he"—*or she*, he might have added, but never had—"is committed to the grave, *and some do not have leave to be settled and still even then....*

PLASTIC MAN

And why should I care what has become of my little brother? Fraternity is a matter of ancestry, after all, and the days of ancestry are dead and gone. Liberty is here at last, and no man need be equal to another. Why should I care that my brother is condemned to be nickel and steel, so that he might exhaust the orgiastic possibilities of magnetism and electricity?

But I do care, for I am a plastic man, and it is in my nature to care.

"I have served my time in the flesh," my brother said to me. "I have studied all the brochures with the utmost care. I have weighed the multitudinous kinds of otherflesh and found them wanting."

"As any sensible man is bound to do," I assured him. "Are we men or are we mice?"

Not one of our grandparents or uncles had ever chosen a life of otherflesh, save for Great-Uncle Unmentionable, the black sheep of the family, who forsook thought altogether and became a great white shark because he felt that intellect and emotion were not reconcilable at all.

"I have considered plastic too," he assured me, "and I am not convinced by its claims."

Not convinced by its claims! Not convinced by the testimony of a once-beloved, once-respected elder brother! Not convinced by the writings of a thousand poets and novelists, nor the greatest philosophers of our age! What has the cause of steel and nickel to put forward in opposition? Even gold and precious stones have their poets, of a sort, but magnetism has nothing at all but bluster, bravado and superficial brightness. Why could he not see it?

"The greatest philosophers of our age," he told me, "are the brains that float in fluid, untroubled by any kind of flesh. They and they alone are creatures of pure reason, free from the sensations of any kind of embodiment. The plastic men who call themselves philosophers are merely mental gymnasts—sophists, if you will. How can anyone trust them, who is not himself a thing of plastic, perfectly content with softness and flexibility, with the unceasing ebb and flow of color and texture, without even the possibility of fixity?"

Oh, how he wounded me with his darts and barbs! Not carelessly either, but with malice in mind. And I his brother, who wanted nothing for him but the best, the finest, the most subtle!

"He who despises softness despises love," I told him. "The one advantage of beginning life as flesh is that we all learn love. Yes, the flesh is terribly weak; yes, the range of fleshy emotion is as narrow as the visual spectrum within the vaster spectrum of possible radiation—but even flesh facilitates love, of a sort. What would be the use of all those crude hormones that natural selection provided, if they did not allow us to glimpse the possibilities of love? And are not the possibilities of love brought to the true perfection by the myriad mutations of plastic? Is not the poetry of the plastic folk the proof and glory of their superiority?"

"Certainly I despise love," he duly informed me. "I have gained nothing from love but pain and confusion. What I have found worthwhile, in the ignominious fraction of possible emotion that flesh provides, is triumph in victory and lust, and the finest possibilities I have glimpsed are those of metal. What can the chemical transactions of organic artificiality offer to compare with the orgasmic surge of electricity, the power of lightning and the swirling cycles of magnetic force? What nobler and intenser feelings can there be? Oh, I am steel, my brother, and have been since the day I learned to walk. How I have longed for the day to come when I could trade my flesh for a body that can truly *feel*—a powerful body, in every sense of the word. What have I ever cared for poetry? The sports-field and the battle-field are the proper testing-grounds of men. You have no idea what a disappointment you have been to me, my brother. How I have wished that you might have set me a better example!"

A lesser man than I would have taken that amiss, but I was a plastic man and could not cease to care. I was a loving brother, who desired to be loved in his turn. Plastic is so much more flexible and versatile than flesh, but I could not easily stand to be despised, or hated. How could I relinquish my fight?

When the day came for my brother to enter the manufactory and complete his rite of passage I was beside him every inch of the way, pleading with him to reconsider his decision—but he would not do it.

In the end, I had to force myself to watch as the doctors of nickel and steel stripped the feeble flesh from his nerves, then multiplied his synapses tenfold before investing them within limbs and a torso of gleaming metal.

How I grieved that night! None but a plastic man really knows the depths and nuances of grief. None but a plastic man retains the plasticity of mind that facilitates true understanding. My brother was lost to me, lost to all the subtleties of the best humanity. He had become a man of action, a man of power, a man of certainty, a man incapable of mere regret.

I was still by his unforgiving bedside when he awoke, but he hardly spared me a glance.

"What do you want with me, plastic man?" he said. "Go home to your own kind, to your softness, to your pale and palliative pleasures."

"We are brothers still," I told him, although I knew that it was not wholly true. He might almost as well have been a shark, having forsaken consciousness altogether in return for the bliss of pure sensation.

"All men are brothers," he assured me, mechanically, "but I am steel and you are not, and such transactions as our various bodies might share are all perverse. Go home, and leave me to discover myself at my leisure. Go home, and forget that you were once flesh, and had a brother that was also flesh. We are ourselves now, not two of a kind."

"It is not in the nature of plastic men to forget," I told him. "How else could we be the conscience of the race, the greatest poets of the age? How can I forget what I have lost along with my frail flesh, when everything I have made of myself cries out for love and fellowship? What would the human race become if there were no plastic men, but only men of steel and copper and otherflesh and lustrous stone?"

"Is that my concern?" he demanded. "I am metal now. I am heir to electrical fire and fury, alive in the only way that is worthwhile. Go home, and live what shadow of life you can. Waste no regrets on me, for I am what I have always wanted and needed to be. I am myself, and proud of it, as only a man can be."

I obeyed. What else could I do?

I had failed, and I had to admit my failure. I had lost, and I had to admit my loss.

I wept, as only a plastic man can weep, and it was the most delicious feeling in the world, finer by far than any electric fire or fury that ever surged in the limbs and heart of a man of steel. Then I made this poem, such as no mere man of metal could ever have forged, nor any mere shark could ever have understood.

What else are mind and progress for, after all, if we cannot draw achievement and delight from the deepest of our dire despairs? We are not made of stone.

APHRODITE AND THE RING

In the catacombs beneath the city of Paris there is an Empire of the Dead: an ossuary into which the ancient cemeteries of the city have been emptied. The fleshless bones are sorted into their different kinds, arrayed partly for convenience and partly for effect. They are ornamented with labels and legends exhorting the visitors who look upon them to remember their own mortality, and recognize that men are but phantoms raised from the dust, who must in time to dust return.

In the vaults beneath the Louvre there is a similar Empire, comprised of the marble fragments of countless shattered statues. Here too the images are sorted into various kinds, arrayed partly for convenience and partly for effect. Here too there are labels and legends to guide the minds of scholars, offering conjectures as to the particular ideas and deities whose phantom existence was long ago made incarnate by credulous and loving artisans.

* * * * * * *

Théophile, the aspirant magician whose destiny it was to bring the ring of betrothal to the severed hand of the goddess of Aphrodite on the thirty-first day of March in the year of Our Lord 1887 was no stranger to either of the Parisian Empires of the Dead, and he felt that he understood them both well enough. With his master Josephin he had often visited the ossuary of Montrouge to gather materials useful in the art of necromancy, and Josephin had brought him to the vaults beneath the Louvre on more than one occasion, in search of the elusive spirit of the miraculous past.

Théophile was confident by now that he knew his way around the storehouses where the relics of the past were kept. Although this was the first time that he had descended alone into the Louvre's vaults he knew exactly what he was looking for. He knew, too, exactly what to do when he found it. He had the magic ring in his pocket, and only needed to place it on the appropriate finger of the appropriate hand in order to obtain his heart's desire.

He had every faith that it would work. He had not the slightest doubt that Josephin's identification of the hand and assessment of its latent virtue were accurate; that Josephin had failed so utterly to identify an untrustworthy apprentice and assess his criminal capability were errors of an altogether different order. Few magicians were as adept in dealing with the everyday world which surrounded them as they were in dealing with the darker world beyond, but in regard to matters magical Josephin had been a true scholar and a true master of arts.

"Magic," Josephin had told him, more by way of self-indulgence than instruction, "is based in hazardous affinity. Unlike science, which deals with the consistent properties that substances have, and which seeks to discover their invariant and reliable laws, magic trades upon the accidental and the ephemeral. Magic is concerned with haphazard points of contact and the arbitrary impositions of the imagination; there is nothing invariant or reliable about it, and all its successes are dependant on the virtues and talents of its practitioners. He who would be a magician must not be content with the study of occult texts; he must bring himself continually into contact with significant relics of the past whose secrets he desires to master, and cultivate a particular sensitivity to its unique meanings and miraculous potentials."

Josephin had thought himself safe in speaking so frankly to a despised apprentice, bought for a few sous. No man of his stripe could ever have believed that a petty servant might have any particular sensitivity to the arcana of his profession, or with the exotic lands of the mythical past. That failure of the imagination killed Master Josephin as surely as the long-bladed dagger that Théophile struck into his heart.

Théophile had no fear that the sudden death of its maker would reduce the magical power that had been so carefully inculcated in the ring that he carried in his pocket; he had cunning enough to know that capture by murderous theft was far more likely to enhance the so-called virtue of a talisman than to reduce it.

Théophile knew exactly where to find the hand; he had looked on while Josephin searched so assiduously for it, and had seen the gleam in his master's eye when it was found. He had taken care to commit every detail of the escapade to memory, even though he had put on a show of skepticism and indifference.

"This is the hand of Aphrodite," Josephin had told him, proudly, three years and a day before.

"Aphrodite has a thousand hands," Théophile had replied, negligently, by way of playing his apprentice part, "and a million broken fingers, if all her ancient images be counted to her credit."

"For every true image," Josephin had retorted, in his lofty and contemptuous fashion, "there are a thousand travesties; for every authentic notion, a million illusions."

Théophile had not replied to that portentous statement then, but he did so now as he laid his lantern down. "In that case," he said, rejoicing in his status as the inheritor of his master's mantle, "let us see what the ring can do to restore the true image and the authentic notion of the goddess Aphrodite."

He took the marble hand from its humble lodging-place, and he slipped the ring out of his pocket. Carefully, he placed the ring on the third finger of the sinister hand. No ceremony or incantation was necessary; the ring and the hand had a ready-made affinity, which only required the appropriate contact to bring it to fruition.

While he held the hand of marble reverently and expectantly in his own, Théophile felt it change.

The hand did not become flesh, but it became animate; it ceased to be a mere representation, and became that which it represented: the hand of Aphrodite.

Théophile brought it to his lips, and kissed the fingers gently.

"This is the work of destiny," he murmured, in a soft and loving voice. "An old man forged the ring, pouring into it the legacy of all his study and discipline, in order that it might breach the boundaries of time and imagination, but what needs Aphrodite of old men? It was surely necessary that a young man should apply the ring, and reap its reward. Who else but a man full of youth and life and strength could draw full benefit from betrothal to the Goddess of Love?"

By the time the apprentice magician finished this gallant speech the hand was no longer disembodied. A naked woman stood before him, whole and entire. He was astonished, as he had known that he would be, but there was something lacking in the tenor of his astonishment. He had expected awesome grandeur and breathtaking beauty, as might befit a Goddess of Love, but....

She was certainly handsome enough, after a fashion, but—to his dire disappointment—not unduly so. Her dark eyes seemed rather dull in the lamplight, her hair was a trifle greasy, her skin was by no means unblemished, her breasts seemed less than firm spite of their stoniness, and her thighs were unfashionably stout. Had she been dressed in ordinary clothing, walking along the Champs Élysées, few heads would have turned to look after her as she went by.

"You have done me a service, Monsieur," she said, pronouncing the words with a noticeable provincial accent. "I thank you kindly for this temporary liberation from oblivion."

After a moment's hesitation, Théophile contrived to say: "Are you truly....?"

"Aphrodite?" she finished for him, seemingly unsurprised but perhaps a trifle offended by his evident skepticism. "The eternal spirit of erotic passion? The unappeasable hunger of the flesh incarnate? The irresistible force of divine madness? Why should you doubt it?"

Why indeed? thought Théophile, sourly. *I have known men who loved creatures shabbier by far than this, with considerable ardor. Why should one expect a goddess of love to be so perfect as to be intimidating? And yet....*

He bent to kiss her hand again, with all the gallantry he could muster. There was, after all, no doubting the supernatural quality of the apparition. The fact that her features were so ordinary did not detract from the miraculousness of her appearance.

"I cannot doubt it," he assured her. "Although it is a marvel beyond any that common men ever encounter, I cannot doubt it."

With a little laugh of delight, she gathered him into her adamantine arms, and her eager fingers began to divest him of his clothing, with an altogether fair degree of skill considering that she could never have encountered a button before. He would rather have taken her away from that gloomy place to somewhere more comfortable, but her enthusiasm was not unflattering (nor did it seem out of character). He capitulated, and put his best efforts into the playing of his own part.

Aphrodite was not unduly cold to the touch, nor even unduly hard, although she certainly had not acquired the texture of ordinary flesh. As she moved against him, while they fondled one another, she seemed to grow more yielding by the minute, and when the time came to consummate their exotic marriage it proved by no means difficult or uncomfortable for him to gain admittance to her inner sanctum. He was glad of that, and grateful to be glad of something, but he was uncomfortably aware that he was not as glad as he had expected to be when he had plunged that triumphant dagger into his master's heart.

In fact, Théophile thought, as the brief affair proceeded all too swiftly to a climax, *it is much the same as lying with any other woman—even a common whore. Was it for this that Josephin labored all his life in the cultivation of his magical affinities? Was it for this that I committed murder?* But he said nothing aloud, and when it was over he continued to stroke his mistress, as affectionately and as reverently as he could. He was not unused to such pretences.

"When all is said and done," he reflected, more by way of casual self-indulgence than attempted explanation, "love is based in the affinities of the flesh. Like magic, it trades upon the accidental and the ephemeral, upon haphazard points of contact and the arbitrary impositions of the imagination; what ought one to expect, therefore, of the true manifestation of a Goddess of Love?"

When a minute or two had passed, seemingly impatient with his unrewarding fumblings, Aphrodite thrust him away.

"Enough," she said. "Eternity beckons and oblivion awaits. One can stand so much of life, love and leisure, but not a moment more. If you have aught to ask, ask it now. Only ask, and I will turn your heart, your flesh and your hopes to cool white stone."

"That is not what I want," replied Théophile, in ill-judged haste.

"As you wish," said the goddess—and left him holding a disembodied hand of marble, now formed into a fist.

There was no possible way of removing the ring from the third finger, but he knew only too well that there would have been nothing to be gained by it anyhow. The virtue had gone out of it now. It was only a ring.

Théophile sighed, wondering what fabulous opportunities—if any—he had lost by replying so intemperately. He stood up stiffly, and dressed himself as quickly as he could. He returned the hand to its lodging-place, wondering whether anyone would ever notice the strange metamorphosis that had taken place. Then he picked up his lantern, and left.

He was not unduly downhearted; after all, he was a magician now. He could not and did not understand that he had summoned from oblivion the Goddess of Love who reflected the qualities of his own dismal soul, and that the kind of magic he now possessed was far less powerful than the kind he might have owned had he been a better kind of man.

* * * * * * *

In the catacombs beneath the city of Paris there is an Empire of the Dead: an ossuary into which the ancient cemeteries of the city have been emptied. The fleshless bones are sorted into their different kinds, arrayed partly for convenience and partly for effect. They are ornamented with labels and legends exhorting the visitors who look upon them to remember their own mortality, and recognize that men are but phantoms raised from the dust, who must in time to dust return. Those who come to gawp and stare read the labels and the legends religiously, and piously believe that they have heard and understood the voice of reason, but they remain obstinately deaf to the true implication of what they have seen.

In the vaults beneath the Louvre there is a similar Empire, comprised of the marble fragments of countless shattered statues. Here too the images are sorted into various kinds, arrayed partly for convenience and partly for effect. Here too there are labels and legends to guide the minds of scholars, offering conjectures as to the particular ideas and deities whose phantom existence was long ago made incarnate by credulous and loving artisans. Those who come to study and marvel proudly believe that they have penetrated the veil of illusion that separates the world of the here and now from the grandeurs of the Golden Age, but they little realize how obdurately blind they are.

DANSE MACABRE

1.

Theoderic Melkarth had been born in the Gothic kingdom established after the fall of Rome—a kingdom whose rulers still retained sufficient vanity in their forefathers' conquest, more than three hundred years after the fact, to regard themselves as the protectors and guides of the heart of the civilized world. Long before he reached his fiftieth year, however, Melkarth had learned that the true heart of contemporary civilization had been located in the Arab lands ever since the decay of Athens and Byzantium and the final destruction of the Library at Alexandria. Although Araby itself was mostly desert, the cluster of emirates surrounding Baghdad still had the benefit of the fertile triangle that had given birth to the primal civilizations of Sumer and Akkad; as the Abbasid dynasty approached its prime, the intellectual hegemony of Mesopotamia was almost fully restored.

Melkarth had discarded his forename long before he became a trusted vizier in the Emirate of Karbala, where his post-Roman wisdom still carried a certain cachet, in cunning alloy with the eastern education that he had very carefully gleaned in Baghdad and Isfahan. He had not entirely discarded the habits of thought that he had formed in his native land, however, although he was exceedingly careful not to display those habits openly. He had lived his life, as most men do, hoping that he would never have to endure disaster, but also with the secret confidence that, if the necessity ever arose, he would be better suited than most men to cope with its vicissitudes.

When the fantastic rumor reached the Emir of Karbala that the djinn which had established themselves as Lords of the Dead in the legendary past had recently returned to the Arab lands in the south and to Egypt in the west, and that they were already raising armies of the resurrected dead, it was only natural that the Emir should entrust his most cosmopolitan vizier and a handful of his colleagues with the important mission of traveling south-westwards with a diplomatic camel-train, in search of further enlightenment regarding the remarkable allegations from emirates closer to the source of the fabulous news.

The camel-train's first intended destination was Tabuk, but the road that would take them there went through Qarah on the northern edge of the An Nafud. The caravan was half a hundred leagues short of Qarah, traveling through sultry evening gloom, when it was attacked by a raiding-party of the risen dead. The attackers were no more than half a hundred strong, but the diplomatic caravan had only a dozen soldiers to guard it and a further dozen servants, most of whom were adolescents incapable of bearing arms.

When the attack began Melkarth was mounted on a milk-white mare, with his servant Syed a little way behind him on a donkey. His fellow vizier, Dwidar al Saad, was on a similar mount to his left, and a brace of guardian soldiers on black stallions flanked their formation, the whole party being somewhat in advance of the line of camels. The raiders, mounted on ungainly but speedy riding-camels, came from the south, emerging from the shadowed sand-dunes a mere few hundred paces away, already galloping full-tilt.

The situation gave the soldiers guarding Melkarth and Dwidar al Saad temporary power of command over their masters, and they instructed their charges to dismount and take shelter while they drew their scimitars and rode off to engage the enemy. At that point, it was impossible for Melkarth to see who or what the attackers were, and his first hopeful assumption, on seeing them clad in tightly-wound white robes, was that they might be mere Bedouin bandits. It was not until the battle, such as it was, had been swiftly concluded, and all the soldiers slain—somewhat artlessly, but very efficiently—that any of the marauders came close enough to his hiding-place to let him see that his optimism had been futile.

The living dead had faces like fleshless skulls—or, at least, skulls with only a thin layer of transparent flesh overlaying them. The only thing that distinguished their visages from the skulls of bodies pecked clean by vultures was that the shadowed orbits of their eyes seemed to contain something solid: not white, like the bulk of the ball of a living man's eye, but definitely solid. Although they were slender, Melkarth judged that they must be considerably stronger and more resilient than living warriors of similar dimension. Even from his distant vantage-point, it had been evident that the mission's defenders had struck numerous blows against their uncanny opponents, but the only skull-face that did not rise to its feet again after the battle had concluded had had its head rudely severed from its shoulders. That one, apparently, was now dead for a second time—but perhaps not irredeemably, for its body was not abandoned, being heaped up with the rest.

The four skull-faced warriors that eventually guided their camels to the place where Melkarth, Dwidar al Saad and Syed were crouching did not dismount and did not speak, but merely beckoned. In the circumstances, Melkarth was glad to see that, for he had fully expected to be slaughtered as casually and definitively as the soldiers had been. He asked the attackers who they were and where they intended taking their prisoners, but he received no reply. "We must go with them meekly," he told Syed, in order that he might continue to pose as a man whose wisdom was relevant, at least in the eyes of his servant. "They have us in their power, and there is no point in resistance."

"Are they truly dead men restored to life by magic?" the boy asked him, evidently trusting that a man a wise as Melkarth would be able to answer that question, as he trusted him to answer all others.

"I cannot be certain," Melkarth admitted, "but they are unlike any living beings I ever saw."

"I've never seen their horrid like either," added Dwidar al Saad, with a shudder, as if doubling the uncertainty somehow increased the sum of their combined knowledge.

Melkarth, Syed and Dwidar al Saad led the two horses and the donkeys to a group of men and beasts that comprised all the human survivors of the raid and their mounts. There were nine in all, comprising five diplomats and four servants; eight servants had been killed along with the soldiers, presumably for having had the temerity to attempt to defend themselves. All of the victims of the unceremonious slaughter had already been gathered into an ominously large heap nearby, in full view of the huddled prisoners, perhaps by way of issuing a warning.

While the captives watched, the shrouded bodies of the dead—including that of the decapitated skull-face—were carefully loaded on to pack-camels, like valuable cargo. The living men whose lives had been preserved, evidently by design, were then instructed by means of gestures to mount their mares and donkeys, while the soldiers' horses were gathered into a string.

"It seems that the Lords of the Dead are keen to collect living slaves as well as dead ones," Melkarth murmured to Dwidar al Saad. "Let us hope that it is the quality of our minds that has recommended us, rather than our mere docility."

"I doubt that they are capable of recognizing quality of mind," his colleague replied, in the tame timid whisper, "and I rather wish that I had had the courage to resist. The poor fellows they have killed are now in paradise, but we might be forced to endure a thousand horrors and ignominies before we join them."

Melkarth nodded his head in reply, but thought that he might yet be capable of enduring a certain amount of horror and ignominy, in the service of his intellectual curiosity—and what ever else the skull-faces might or might not be, they were certainly not uninteresting.

In the days and nights that followed, while the captives were hurried southwards, the soldiers' horses were used in relay with the diplomats' own mounts, but there was a steady attrition as the beasts broke down, and the pace of the strange caravan slowed markedly as it moved deep into Jabal Shammar. Two of the humans died too—one diplomat and one servant—perhaps as much from dread as illness or injury, and were transferred to the cargo borne by the pack-camels.

The dwindling company of living men and their mounts was forced into close proximity while they were on the move in the morning or the evening, but the seven remaining riders would have clustered together anyway, to begin with, so frightened were they of their camel-mounted captors, whose conspicuous inhumanity seemed all the more alarming for the respectful distance they kept from their prey. Horror is a perishable emotion, though, and by the time they had been riding for three days, the skull-faces had come to seem familiar, and even slightly pathetic in their automatism.

They are mere puppets, after all, Melkarth thought, remembering what Dwidar al Saad had said about the souls of the dead soldiers having already taken up residence in paradise. *They are made from human flesh, but they are not human beings; they might as well have been molded out of inanimate clay, or fallen from the moon. They are playthings, pieces in some strange game that a company of djinn has elected to play, according to rules unfathomable to humans.*

It became obvious, as the southbound train encountered more and more parties of skull-faced travelers heading in the opposite direction, that a substantial traffic had already been established between this newly-hatched Empire of the Dead and the Lands of the Living that lay to either side of the Red Sea. Sometimes, when they crested a rise, Melkarth was able to catch a glimpse of a distant dust-cloud stirred up by another group of camels traveling ahead of them, and he deduced that the viziers of Karbala were by no means the only living captives being transported into the reborn Land of the Dead.

When the caravan stopped in the middle of the day or the middle of the night, the captive diplomats were given a tent of their own, and served food from their own supplies, but they had little enough opportunity to examine their skeletal captors at close range, or to attempt further communication on the subject of where they were being taken or why. They had no option but to fall back upon the rumors that had brought them forth from Karbala in the first place, which now seemed to have been promoted from the humble rank of fanciful travelers' tales to that of dire intelligence of doom to come.

The chief purveyor of these tales among the seven, whose place of birth was as far to the east of Baghdad as Melkarth's was to the west, was a dark man named Zainul Abedin, who claimed descent from the followers of Zoroaster and privileged knowledge of the ancient mysteries of that sect. He had won a promotion in esteem following their capture, from undiscriminating rumor-monger to possible authority on the society and politics of the renascent Empire of the Dead.

"The legend says that the Lords of the Dead were rebels even among the djinn," Zainul Abedin told his companions in misfortune, one day when they were becalmed by a sandstorm while still sufficiently unexhausted to hold an extensive conversation, "and were considered insane by their own kind, the majority of which did not mourn their eventual banishment—but it was the One True God who contrived that banishment, by means of his prophet Suleiman the Magnificent."

"We all know the story, although its details have been blurred by the centuries," said Dwidar al Saad. "The point is, how and why have the Lords of the Dead returned?"

In fact, Melkarth was not very familiar with the story, having been born in the west, where Suleiman was known as Solomon and was primarily feted for his skill in settling disputes regarding motherhood. He was quick to raise that objection—which gave Zainul Abedin, who had always been jealous of Melkarth's higher status in the Emir's court, considerable pleasure.

"Suleiman the Magnificent tricked the king of the djinn, Azazel, into surrendering a secret by means of which Azazel's subject djinn were bound and imprisoned for a thousand years," Zainul Abedin explained. "The details have become hazy over time, as Dwidar al Saad observes, but Suleiman took advantage of a passion for gaming that the Lords of the Dead had, which had provoked them to make their armies of the dead in the first place. Suleiman tempted Azazel into an unwise wager, which won him a prize whose potential value Azazel had not suspected."

"Some say that Azazel lost the wager deliberately," Alkadi al Medoun put in, "because he knew that a party of rival djinn had secretly assisted Suleiman in framing its terms, but that Suleiman the Wise cheated both parties; Azazel was not bound and imprisoned, as his rivals hoped, nor were the djinn who helped Suleiman, as Azazel had hoped, but Azazel's immediate followers, the Lords of Death, were put away."

"Azazel was the most hideous tyrant the world has ever known," Zainul Abedin hastened to say, annoyed by the interruption, "and the djinn of his strange company ruled a dread empire of human beings long before there was any human-ruled empire in the world. The Land of the Dead had as many living inhabitants as dead ones, who labored under a double curse, knowing that they could not be released from their misery even by death, for they would have to endure a second term of agonizing servitude thereafter, doing the work of the ultimate enemies of humankind. This was an insult to the One True God, whose prophet Suleiman was—like Zoroaster before him and Mohammed more recently—and it was Allah, not rival djinn, who enabled Suleiman to defeat the Lords of the Dead."

Dwidar al Saad nodded in response to this judgment, and Alkadi al Medoun was obliged to put on a show of contrition; even Melkarth was careful to retain a pose of interested and non-judgmental enquiry.

"The One True God has dominion over the souls of the dead," Zainul Abedin continued, now confident of having the floor entirely to himself for a while, "and He was offended by the game of dispossession and reanimation that Azazel's followers had begun to play with the husks in which souls are clad during their Earthly existence. He empowered Suleiman to free the living from their enslavement to the vile djinn of the Land of the Dead, and to let the reclad bones of the dead rest in peace. Suleiman was granted the means to defeat Azazel by guile, because that is the djinn's greatest vulnerability. Their magic gives them power, but they are fundamentally unintelligent.

"The cleverness with which Allah endowed him enabled Suleiman to win an opportunity to deploy the Great Seal, which bears the One True God's unspeakable Secret Name. The use of the Seal allowed him to bind the unruly djinn in caverns within the earth, or trap them in bottles that were hurled into the sea. It is said that Azazel escaped, but became a pariah among his own kind as a result of his ignominious defeat; none of the djinn of other lands would give him refuge.

"The djinn of other lands had not enslaved humans in the same fashion, and were glad they had refrained when they saw what the One True God had sent Suleiman to do; those which hated human-kind continued to express their enmity in subtler ways, but none ever dared to set themselves up as brutal tyrants of the same sort."

"Until now, it seems," muttered Alkadi al Medoun.

Dwidar al Saad and Zainul Abedin frowned, but Melkarth was quick to intervene. "Alkadi al Medoun makes an interesting point," he said, "but the rumors that reached the Emir said that the djinn who were once the Lords of the Dead had returned, not that others had taken up the same game. If that is true, does it mean that Suleiman's Seal has lost its effect?"

"Impossible," Zainul Abedin was quick to judge. "It is unthink-able that the Great Seal has simply *lost its effect*. What must have happened is that someone—perhaps a human, but more likely a djinni—has found a cunning means of liberating at least some of the djinn that Suleiman imprisoned, without breaking the Seals that held them captive. Doubtless the One True God will appoint a new prophet soon enough, to renew and reinforce Suleiman's work—but in the meantime, honest and worthy men like us will be obliged to suffer pain, humiliation and death, as a punishment for the wicked-ness to which our fellows have surrendered themselves, thus cor-rupting the society that ought to have been obedient to the Law of God."

Melkarth was not so sure that he, let alone any of his less august colleagues, was entitled to number themselves among the uncor-rupted, but he held his tongue on that score, as was his duty of po-liteness, and thanked Zainul Abedin for the enlightenment and food for thought that he had provided.

2.

As the little caravan continued on its way, it seemed to be mak-ing good progress, for it gradually gained on the larger camel-train that was heading for the same destination a little way ahead of the viziers of Karbala. Melkarth hoped that the two companies might eventually meet and merge, because he was interested to see other prisoners that the skull-faces had taken the trouble to capture alive. He could not be certain, as yet, whether he had been captured because he was a wise man, whose knowledge and intelligence might be of some use to the djinn who posed as Lords of the Dead, or whether he had simply advertised his tractability by putting up no resistance. The answer to that question, he knew, might make a considerable difference to his eventual fate, and the possibility of his reaping any further rewards from life.

The journey was arduous, but not so hard as to amount to torture. The seven prisoners were regularly fed and given enough water to prevent their perpetual thirst turning to agony. They were not forced to march in the fiercest heat of the day, nor in the darkest hours of the night, although it seemed to Melkarth that the skull-faces were not much troubled by hunger, thirst, heat or darkness. They did eat and drink, just as they clothed and hooded themselves against the glare of the sun and the sting of windblown sand, but they seemed to be considerably more patient, resilient and resolute than living men. Once they became so familiar to their captives that their appearance no longer provoked frissons of horror and dread, it became possible to wonder whether their estate was so very undesirable. They were, to be sure, bodies from which the souls had undoubtedly fled, but Melkarth felt free to speculate that they might nevertheless retain some vestiges of self-awareness and intelligent thought, just as they retained the capacity to nourish themselves and act with purpose. If so, was it not conceivable that they might not be entirely discontented with their lot?

Similar thoughts seemed to be stirring in the minds of his colleagues. "When I heard tales of the resurrected dead in my childhood," Alkadi al Medoun confessed, during one of their nocturnal conversations, "I always imagined them as shambling creatures, grey in color and reeking of decay, which thirsted after human blood and were wont to devour their prey. In fact, they are quite different."

The oldest of the surviving servants, whose name was Hamdan, exhibited a boldness that would have been intolerable in any other circumstances by providing an addendum to this remark. "I had always imagined the dead who linger on Earth to be wraiths," he said, "more vaporous than solid, invisible in sunlight but palely manifest by night—but these are indeed quite different."

"The risen dead are said to be of numerous species," Zainul Abedin told them loftily. "Those which have captured us belong to one of those recognized types. I have only seen our captors fully-clad, as yet, but the lore of legend suggests that what little flesh they have is all as transparent as the flesh on their faces—save, of course, for the black orbs of their eyes and their worm-like tongues. Their hearts and stomachs are said to be black too, and there are gauze-like networks of some sort within their torsos and abdomens. The fact that they are so careful not to show themselves bespeaks a modesty of sorts, or a sense of shame. They are miserable creatures, extremely stupid by comparison with living men, but they are not entirely insensitive, in spite of their murderousness."

"They are not as stupid as they seem at first glance," Dwidar al Saad said, pensively. "They cannot talk, it seems, but the sign-language they use is not unsophisticated."

"They do not talk to us in Arabic," Alkadi al Medoun observed, "but we cannot be sure that they have no spoken language for use among themselves."

"There are philosophers among the living," Zainul Abedin put in, still enthusiastic to pose as a knowledgeable scholar rather than a mere rumor-monger, "who consider the Arabic language to be the particular gift of the One True God to His most faithful devotees. If the resurrected dead can speak among themselves, they must be obliged to use the language of the djinns, which is more primitive than the most barbarous residues of the curse of Babel. That lack deprives the djinn and the dead alike of the privileges of beautiful and wise expression."

"Do you think, my lord, that there is any prospect of our being rescued?" Hamdan asked Melkarth, further emboldened by the lack of any violent reaction to his earlier intrusion and now apparently certain that shared captivity had narrowed the gap between his status and that of his masters.

Before Melkarth could answer, Zainul Abedin spoke again, with ostentatious condescension. "We who have faith in the One True God may be certain that another prophet will be sent to follow in the steps of the great Mohammed, if necessity requires his dispatch, but we cannot know when."

"Hamdan is thinking in simpler terms than that," Melkarth said, gently. "Alas, I doubt that any living army will come from Karbala or any other stronghold of civilization in time to rescue us from conscription into the army of the dead—but we must not give up hope. Any attempt to escape would be futile while we are deep in an unknown desert, but we do not know what opportunities the future might bring. We have been taken alive, and our captors must intend to keep us alive for a while longer, else they would have killed us. While there is life there is hope."

"We are educated men," Dwidar al Saad observed, presumably excluding Hamdan and the other servants from the generalization. "Our knowledge of the present state of the world might be of considerable use to our captors, if they really have been imprisoned or asleep for a thousand years and more. Many generations of men have come and gone in that interim, and we have made considerable progress in the arts and sciences. If the resurrected dead have lost their knowledge along with their souls, the particular Lord of the Dead whom our captors serve might think it well worth his while to keep us alive for as long as possible—don't you agree, Melkarth?"

"It seems not unlikely," Melkarth said, judiciously, "that we shall remain alive as long as our lives are considered useful."

"We would be traitors to the One True God," Zainul Abedin said, flatly, "if we were to put our hard-won wisdom at the disposal of rebel djinn. It is our duty to remain stubbornly silent, no matter what might be done to us to make us speak."

That opinion imposed a dreadful silence on the little company. Not one of its number, in Melkarth's judgment, was likely to hold his tongue under the lightest or torture—which made the thought that they might be obliged by their faith to try seem even more chilling. As a westerner, though, with as much Roman blood in him as Gothic, Melkarth had already consented to make a gift of his wisdom to an alien king. Was the notion of substituting a curious djinni for the Emir of Karbala really as horrifying and as blasphemous as his fellow viziers claimed to find it?

"Why did the djinn of the legendary Land of the Dead reanimate slaves, I wonder, when the djinn of other lands, whatever evil they might do in others ways, never dabble in such black arts?" Alkadi al Medoun asked. Melkarth assumed that he was deliberately changing the subject.

"They were prudent masters," Hamdan suggested, before Zainul Abedin could make any further show of his expertise. "If one can get twice as much work from a servant by means of black magic, why discard him when he's only part way through his useful existence?"

"It was because the dead made better slaves than the living," Zainul Abedin put in, quick to reclaim his prerogative as a fount of apparent wisdom. "They're more tractable and more durable. It is against the Law of Allah for djinn to make slaves of human beings, though—even human beings whose souls have departed their bodies—and the Lords of the Dead were punished for their presumption, to set an example to the rest."

But now their term of punishment is at an end, it seems, Melkarth thought.

The diplomats' journey eventually came to its terminus in a city forged in stone, whose ruins must have been buried in the desert sands for centuries but whose surviving foundations had now been swept clean of all but drifting dust. As they approached a gate in its reconstructed wall, they finally caught up with the larger camel-train that had been traveling ahead of them, but there was no opportunity for any fraternization between the two groups of living prisoners, who were kept separate when they had passed through the gate, made to stand still, a hundred paces apart, while the cargoes of the two trains were divided up. This did not prevent Melkarth from studying the other group of prisoners carefully, trying to measure their quality.

There were twenty of them, in all, and none of them was costumed as an aristocrat, let alone as a scholar—which was a bitter disappointment to the vizier, who was still hoping that it was his scholarship that had won him a reprieve from immediate recruitment to the legions of the dead. He realized, however, after a few moments' intense study, that he had seen at least one of them before.

The man who was doing his best to reassure his frightened companions, tacitly assuming leadership of the band, was an acrobat of some celebrity—part of a traveling troupe that moved back and forth between the northern Emirates, entertaining their courts. Once he had recognized the first man, the faces of several of the others struck chords in his memory. One of them, an unveiled female of considerable beauty, was surely a dancer named Zelome, who had entranced the Emir when the troupe had performed in Karbala only a few weeks before the diplomatic mission had set out. Nor was the recognition all one-way—when the leader of the other band saw him staring, the acrobat was quick to salute, and then set about nudging all his fellows, pointing out the party of viziers.

He is glad to see us, Melkarth thought. *Our presence gives him renewed courage, because he knows that we are wise men and thinks that we might be able achieve something on behalf of our captured fellows. I only hope that he is right!*

He directed his attention then to the populace of the city. Thousands of skull-faced workers were toiling, apparently tirelessly, to restore the wall and the nearer edifices. They were working under the supervision of overseers of more varied sorts, but the overseers seemed merely to be organizing the labor rather than compelling its accomplishment with shouts and blows, as overseers in Karbala were routinely obliged to do.

The greater number of the original stone blocks that had framed the city's palaces and public dwellings had evidently survived the centuries, although the buildings had collapsed. Much of the ongoing work was a straightforward, though rather complex, process of reassembly. The wood and fabrics that had completed the environment of the ancient civilization had long decayed into dust, however, and would have to be replaced. Camel-trains were evidently busy already bringing such materials into the city, for a distribution-center of sorts had been set up within the gates, where items of many sorts were in the process of being stored and sorted.

Such caravans would obviously be obliged to travel long distances, but Melkarth caught glimpses of goods within the warehouses that must have been gathered from far and wide, perhaps from as far afield as Ethiopia and India. Even so, he had to suppose that restoring softer surfaces and supplements to the city's imperishable stones would be an exceedingly long and tedious task. Like the resurrected dead themselves, this reborn fragment of the Land of the Dead was, as yet, a scantily clad skeleton, which retained no more than an echo of its former flesh.

There were no shambling ghouls or insubstantial wraiths in the streets of the strange Necropolis, of the kinds that Alkadi al Medoun and Hamdan had mentioned, but there were some living men mingled with the skull-face laborers, mostly serving as overseers, and there were also monsters of other sorts, which did not seem to be involved in the work of reconstruction but involved themselves in the business of the warehouses.

Melkarth was very interested to observe these creatures, which mostly had humanoid bodies fully dressed in pulp flesh and brown skin, but had the heads of animals, most commonly jackals, cats and hawks. He had seen representations of beings of these sorts in Egyptian statuary and tomb-paintings, but had always thought them purely hypothetical images of false gods, or priests equipped with ornamental head-dresses. There was no doubt that the strange beings in the city of the dead were authentic chimeras, however. Like the skull-faces, they seemed to have no spoken language, but they were obviously able to communicate fluently with their living and skeletal colleagues by means of subtle signs and gestures.

The camel-train that had brought the viziers to the city was swiftly broken up. The pack-camels carrying the dead soldiers—whose reek of putrefaction had already become intolerable—were led away towards the eastern quarter of the city, presumably to the place of where the dead men's bodies would be reanimated. The other beasts of burden were taken in the opposite direction, and the horses were carefully stabled on either side of the gate.

The four viziers and the three servants were then guided on foot through the streets towards a central palace-complex, whose imposing towers were already reaching high into the sky, although they were not yet quite complete. They walked slowly, for the morning sun was high in the sky and the heat would have been oppressive even if the air had not been laden with so much pale dust. The two skull-faces appointed to guide them did not try to hurry them along, although they seemed as strong and resolute as ever in themselves.

"The architecture of these constructions is utterly barbarous," Alkadi al Medoun remarked, as they made their way to the heart of the Necropolis. "There is not a minaret or a Greek arch to be seen anywhere, nor is there the slightest indication of artful tiling."

"That's true," Melkarth agreed. "What leaps to my eye, though, is that none of the overseers guiding the skull-faces in their work of reconstruction is carrying a whip."

"The dead certainly seem to work willingly," Zainul Abedin agreed. "That is a measure of the absolute quality of their enslavement."

"Their living companions seem to be working willingly too," Melkarth observed. "Perhaps not entirely by choice, though."

"The djinn are powerful magicians" said Alkadi al Medoun, ominously. "They must have more than one way of guaranteeing absolute obedience—and they have more than one manner of playing games with human flesh. Humans who prove resistant to their subtle modes of compulsion evidently have their heads replaced by more submissive ones."

"While still alive, if appearances can be trusted," Zainul Abedin said, pensively. "I wonder what happens to their heads."

"We must hope that their souls are freed," murmured Dwidar al Saad, very anxiously. "To have one's head chopped off and one's self-awareness perpetuated therein would be a fate even worse than eternal toiling slavery."

"We must not lose hope," said Alkadi al Medoun, desperately. "As faithful followers of the One True God, we have a future in Paradise, and if we must suffer a delay in reaching it, we must bear that delay as patiently as we can. As Melkarth says, while we still live we have hope."

Melkarth observed his fellow viziers and the three servants as they reacted to this suggestion, and saw that any hope they had contrived to conserve thus far was fast ebbing away as they watched hundreds of skull-faces moving hither and yon like dull automata, with animal-headed chimeras drifting between them. Young Syed, he felt sure, must imagine that he was already in hell, and damned.

"We must not despair," he said, dutifully supporting Alkadi al Medoun. "We must look upon this as an opportunity to learn all that we can about the risen dead and their masters. Let us not forget that they were defeated once, by the guile of a man. Like every great prophet, Suleiman has left a legacy of hope behind him for other men to draw upon. We are alive, and it is our task now—viziers and servants alike—to represent the living in this new Land of the Dead, as explorers, diplomats and spies."

"In the Far East," Dwidar al Saad said, thoughtfully, "people believe that the soul is continually reincarnated, until it achieves an enlightenment that allow it the ultimate bliss of oblivion. Their philosophers declare that the duration of a life is an irrelevance, all that really matters being the manner of its progress from one incarnation to the next. Such men as those might not be averse to the kind of resurrection practiced by the Lords of Death. Perhaps the returned djinn might be welcome there—perhaps at least, we might attempt to persuade them of it, and make the suggestion that they build their new empire elsewhere."

"Unless, of course," Hamdan muttered, "their principal purpose is to annoy and torment us. They're masters, after all." No one scolded him for his temerity, or the naked insult in his words.

"It is the duty of the faithful to fight the armies of the risen dead as best they can, in whatever circumstances they find themselves," said Zainul Abedin firmly—although he did not seem entirely confident in making the statement, perhaps because he had been surrounded by the risen dead for some time, and had not yet lifted a finger to resist them. "We must all resist the Lords of Death with the means at our disposal, less they lead all humankind to damnation."

"In that case," said Melkarth, mildly, "we must hope that we have the strength of will to resist imperious resurrection as well as the interrogations of our captors. Let us ask Allah for the strength to resist any magic that might compel us to collaborate in this horrid cause—including the magic of resurrection, in order that our bodies might remain stubbornly dead once we have been killed and our souls have departed therefrom."

"I have grown used to the idea of the skull-faced automata," Dwidar al Saad remarked, dully, "but I do not want my head ripped off, to be replaced by a jackal's. That would be too much."

"The greater threat might lie in being allowed to remain alive and whole, but obliged by entrancement to be loyal servants of the Lords of Death," Zainul Abedin said. "Do you not think so, Lord Melkarth?"

Melkarth cursed his colleague silently for undermining his attempts to maintain morale, but he could not entirely conceal his own anxiety. "It would be unfortunate," he admitted, "to be compelled by subtle magic to imagine the reanimated dead as natural and good, and their murderous crusade against the living as the entirely natural intercourse of the dead-but-active and the active-but-not-yet-dead, by which the former attempt to embrace the latter and initiate them into the mysteries of their own condition. Let us hope that we shall be able to remain devoted followers of the One True God, in life and in death, and will never allow ourselves to be convinced that the crusade now being waged by the Lords of Death is not a genocidal war, but merely a matter of enthusiastic reproduction."

Melkarth's fellow viziers stared at him in horror as the implications of this speech slowly sank in, and Melkarth regretted having made it, even though he had felt it incumbent on him to spell out his darker fears.

3.

The living overseer to whom the prisoners were consigned by their silent captors, when they were finally moved into the shadows of the central palace-complex, was entirely human in form—but Melkarth was unable to take much comfort from that, given the suggestions he had just put to his companions. The man was not only capable of speech but had no difficulty at all expressing himself in fluent Arabic as he bowed to the viziers and bid them welcome, informing them that his name was Tahir and that he had formerly been a native of Damascus. Immediately thereafter, by means of an abrupt gesture of his right hand, Tahir ordered the skull-faces who had escorted the party to the palace to take the three servants away again.

"You must not take our servants away," Melkarth protested. "We are diplomats, special envoys of the Emir of Karbala, and must be treated with respect."

"You will be provided with servants appropriate to your position," Tahir replied, while Syed, Hamdan and the third boy—whose name was Elaq—were led away.

Melkarth studied Tahir carefully, trying to judge whether he was acting freely or under compulsion, but he could not tell. Reluctantly, he introduced himself and his three companions by name, and reiterated his insistence that they were entitle to the respect due to philosophers and ambassadors of the Court of Karbala. "May I know the name of the king whose servant you are, and what rank you hold in his service?" he concluded

"The Lord of the Dead whom I am honored to serve is Cimejez," Tahir replied, "who is himself loyal to Zelebsel, the Supreme Lord of Death and the architect of the Great Awakening."

"Honored to serve?" Dwidar al Saad echoed, ignoring Melkarth's displeasure at the breach of protocol. "How can a living man be honored to serve a djinni? Surely you must be bound to that service by some powerful spell."

Tahir merely bowed, and said: "You will understand in due course, my lord, the terms under which the living give service to the Lords of the Dead."

"May we meet this Cimejez, in order that we might offer the respects of the Emir of Karbala and the Abbasids of Baghdad?" Melkarth asked.

"Indeed you may," Tahir replied. "When you are bathed, rested and refreshed you will be summoned—very soon, I think, for I know that my lord has long anticipated a meeting with men of your sort, and is anxious to converse with you. He is a philosopher himself, of unusual distinction among the djinn. A thousand years ago, before the treachery of Azazel and his minion Suleiman, Cimejez kept the finest court in the Land of the Dead; he was the first patron among the djinn of human astronomy, alchemy and mathematics. It was a tragedy of inestimable proportions that his efforts in the cause of human civilization were thwarted by the aggressive envy of un-worthier rivals."

Melkarth was not unduly surprised by this speech; in the Emir-ates too, custom demanded that a servant should heap fulsome praise on his master in formal situations, especially in his master's own house—but he did not want to waste time with absurd ceremonies that might make the situation seem more ordinary that it was. "That, I fear, is a story that has been oft repeated while your master has been away," he murmured. "Many of the great cities in which those arts have been preserved and improved have fallen to the envious violence of barbarian hordes as the centuries have passed."

"Inevitably so," said Tahir, with an ostentatious sigh. "Without benevolent djinn like my master Cimejez to guide and protect them, the humans of these desert regions must have had few opportunities to rise above their infinitesimal God-given status."

Melkarth could not help being startled by that blasphemy, and he heard more than one of his colleagues draw in their breath sharply, but he was a diplomat of long experience, and knew how to hide his astonishment in circumstances such as these. "There is no God but Allah," he quoted, dutifully.

"That is the God I mean," Tahir replied, with equanimity. "The creator of humankind, and perhaps of the world on which we stand—but not of the djinn."

"The djinn," Melkarth observed, "are generally believed by men to be enemies of the creator of mankind."

"Indeed they are," Tahir agreed, "without exception—although those who aspire to be the saviors of humankind from the inconven-iences of their situation are by no means a majority within the com-pany of the djinn. The Lords of the Dead were few in number even before the treachery of Azazel, and are fewer still at present, but you are privileged to be guest of the kindliest of them all in Cimejez."

Melkarth heard Zainul Abedin mutter a sentence that included the phrase *traitor to the living*, but when he put his hand on his col-league's arm the other fell silent.

"If you will forgive the observation," Melkarth said, "your mas-ter's soldiers did not seem unduly kind when they assailed our cara-van. They killed a dozen men-at-arms and almost as many unarmed servants—and one of our own tiny company of wise men died during the long and arduous journey south."

"The kindness of the Lords of Death is sometimes hard for humans—even humans as wise as you—to recognize," Tahir admitted, with a note of studied regret in his voice, "but you will learn to understand and appreciate it soon enough, as I have done. May I show you to your quarters now, in order that you might recover from your long and arduous journey?"

Melkarth nodded his head with due ceremonious exaggeration, and carefully refrained from interrogating Tahir further, even though he was very curious to know what the man's reasons were for pledging allegiance—as he plainly had done, apparently of his own free will—to a Lord of Death.

Tahir led the four viziers to what must have been one of the smaller apartments in the vast stone edifice, which they found to be crudely but not uncomfortably furnished. Although the chairs were austerely functional and there were no sofas, the carpets were plush and the beds not unduly hard. The baths were mere stone troughs, but they were capacious. What attracted Melkarth's curiosity most of all, however, was the decorative wall-hangings. The tapestry-work was primitive and the designs crude as well as blasphemous—they were not dissimilar to Egyptian tomb-paintings in their representations of human and part-human individuals—but they seemed to have been recently produced, perhaps for the specific purpose of attempting to make educated visitors feel "at home".

"Are these quarters satisfactory?" Tahir asked, opening the door to further questions.

"They would be far more satisfactory," Melkarth said, "if we had our servants with us to attend to our needs."

Tahir clapped his hands, and seven servants immediately filed into the apartment. They bowed to the viziers as soon as they had lined up before them. All but two of them were skull-faces of relatively short stature; the exceptions were living females hardly past puberty.

"Rintrah and Aharia," said Tahir, by way of introduction—he evidently did not think it necessary to give the skull-faces names.

"They can relay spoken orders to their companions." He bowed again and withdrew, without asking permission.

"How long have you been here, Rintrah?" Melkarth asked the older of the two living servants.

"I don't know, Master," the girl replied, in slightly barbarous Arabic.

"Where do you come from?"

"I don't know, Master."

Further questions only served to demonstrate that both servants were dull of mind and sensation alike, and seemed to have no memories of their former lives. Unlike Tahir, they were very obviously subject to some kind of spell—but they were capable of taking orders, relaying instructions to the skull-faces and answering simple questions with regard to the organization and equipment of the apartment. About Cimejez and his city they apparently knew nothing—or, at least, were quite unable to say what they knew.

"Oh well," said Dwidar al Saad, sadly. "At least they don't have the heads of cats. I can bear the skull-faces now, I think."

"Rintrah," said Melkarth, "will you order one of the silent servants to undress, so that we might see its body." He was not certain that it was a permissible request, but the girl made the requisite signs without any reluctance.

Zainul Abedin clicked his tongue in satisfaction as he saw that his earlier claims were mostly borne out. All the flesh that lay upon the skeleton of the dead human—whose sex was impossible to judge—was transparent, but the heart and stomach were as black as the eyes and tongue. There was indeed a network of thin dark lines emerging from the heart to spread through the body, in which a colorless fluid appeared to be moving.

"Remarkable," Melkarth commented. "Thank you—you may readjust your dress." He spoke directly to the skull-face, but it was not until Rintrah had made the requisite gestures that the instruction was followed. The servants were then dismissed.

"I was right about everything, you see," Zainul Abedin was quick to claim. "The lore of legend is reliable. The Lords of the Dead have returned, and they are eager for revenge. They do not hesitate to declare themselves openly as enemies of Allah. Our bodies and souls alike are in dire peril. The best we can hope for is to die quickly and cleanly, so that our souls will be transmitted to paradise while our bodies are subject whatever future degradation they might be forced to undergo."

"The essential points of your legendary narrative appear to be correct, if Tahir can be trusted," Melkarth conceded, "but let us not rush to martyrdom. There is much to learn before we decide how to make our stand on behalf of righteousness."

"That's true," Alkadi al Medoun was quick to say.

"And we are scholars, after all," Dwidar al Saad put in, obligingly. "Our first duty to the One True God, in that capacity, is to learn what we can about his adversaries, in the hope that we might put it to good use in frustrating their satanic cause."

"But we must not give away information that might be useful to enemy armies," Zainul Abedin said, a trifle querulously. "We must not tell this Cimejez anything that might help his campaign of vengeance."

"Absolutely not," said Dwidar al Saad.

"We must not allow ourselves to be seduced, as this Tahir seems to have been seduced, to the enemy's cause" added Alkadi al Medoun

"Agreed," said Melkarth, making the private judgment that Cimejez would not need to be unduly forceful or unduly clever, to persuade his companions to spill every detail of useful knowledge they might possess. "But if we are to be strong, and clever in our intelligence-gathering, we must restore our bodies and our minds to a proper state of health—so let us take full advantage of the facilities we have been offered."

4.

The summons from Cimejez was not long in coming, and Melkarth was not displeased to receive it so soon, having formed a strong curiosity to see a djinni in the flesh—assuming, as he did, that a Lord of the Dead did consent to wear flesh, rather than maintaining a contemptuous invisibility, as the djinn of Mesopotamia and their demonic cousins in the west were reputedly wont to do.

As soon as he and his companions were ushered into the throne-room, Melkarth perceived that the Lords of the Dead had remade their servants in his own image, or perhaps *vice versa*. As was only appropriate, however, the ex-human skull-faces were a little smaller than their model; Cimejez, in his present incarnation, was approximately eight feet tall. The robes he wore, although intricate in their tailoring, were transparent, evidently having been designed to display his remarkable flesh. Melkarth was able to confirm that the details he had observed in his newly-acquired servant were evidently typical. Like the humblest of his skull-faces, Cimejez had a black heart and stomach, but of more majestic proportions. The network of vessels expanding from his heart was similarly blurred, but easier to distinguish by virtue of its larger scale.

The sight of the djinni was so fascinating that Melkarth barely found time to glance around the large, high-ceilinged room, but he made the effort. The capacious floor-space was bare of furniture, save for the large and crudely angular throne, which was set upon a plinth some three feet high. This allowed Cimejez to look down upon his visitors, even though he was seated and they were forced to stand. The floor was made of plain stone blocks, reasonably close-fitted but not devoid of gaping cracks. The walls were painted with large-scale images similar to those on the hangings in the viziers' apartment, depicting humans and chimeras in stiff and awkward poses, in company with various instruments and containers of a con-spicuously primitive sort.

Why should its decoration not resemble an Egyptian tomb? Melkarth thought. *Is not this entire city a tomb of sorts: a veritable metropolis of the dead?*

Tahir introduced the four viziers by name, indicating by subtle gestures that Melkarth was the senior figure among them, and then withdrew. The result of this advertisement was that it was Melkarth whom Cimejez chose to study most intently with his enigmatic eyes, and Melkarth to whom he addressed his own very elaborate but rather condescending welcome.

"I am glad to welcome you here, Ambassadors of Karbala," the Lord of Death informed his guests, loftily—confirming that at least some creatures of his extraordinary sort were not only capable of speech but fluent in Arabic. "My dutiful servants have been able to gather common people to swell their ranks in amazing abundance—nomad tribesmen, crop-growers, soldiers, bandits and the like—but educated men have been hard to find, thus far. The Great Awakening is only just beginning, as you have doubtless observed, but it is making better headway than we could ever have expected, thanks to the increase in human numbers that has taken place since the treason of Azazel. I wish that I still had all the treasures of my former realm to show you, in order that you would be able to take the measure of my intellect and taste more accurately, but those that were immune to vulgar decay have been long dissipated by thieves. I hope that you will be able to help me recover, replace and augment my stock. I shall provide you with scribes as soon as I have some to offer, so that you may begin to make a full record of the wisdom of recent ages, and I hope that you will be able to advise my agents as to where they might lay their hands on precious manuscripts to supplement that library, as well as astronomical instruments and alchemical resources."

"I wish that I could tell you that we are delighted to be here, my lord," Melkarth replied, refusing to be intimidated by the djinni's alarming appearance or overwhelmed by his enthusiasm; fortunately, he was no stranger to the egotism of rulers, nor to its expression in bizarre pomp and garrulity. "Alas, I cannot. Had you sent emissaries to my master, the Emir of Karbala, he might have agreed to send a party of diplomats to your court, but I feel obliged to register our disapproval of your sending soldiers to slaughter the guards who were escorting us on a very different mission to another Emir. That is not the way that civilized individuals conduct their affairs."

"I am grateful for your honesty, Melkarth," Cimejez replied, in a voice whose words were perfectly lucid, although its tone was strangely difficult to interpret, "just as I shall be grateful, in due course, for your understanding and collaboration. When the Land of the Dead was in its heyday, its Emperors did sent emissaries to neighboring lands, but they were not often received in friendly fashion. Am I to understand that humans have made such progress in the meantime that all violence and war have been abolished from the society of nations, and that a diplomatic mission of the risen dead would have been received in Karbala with all due courtesy and ceremony?"

Melkarth was not entirely sure whether Cimejez was being sarcastic or not, but thought it most prudent to assume that he was. "I admit that such a mission might have run into certain difficulties, my lord," he said, smoothly, "and you are entirely right to lament the fact that, even in the very heart of human civilization, men are still too often wont to settle their disputes violently. Even so, I feel compelled to make the observation that it is a little unfair to chide us for not having abolished violence and warfare, when you are so eager to slaughter the living and enslave their reanimated corpses."

"I forgive your mistake," Cimejez retorted, "and I shall do my very best to ensure that achieve a far better understanding of my nature and purpose in reshaping and remaking your fellow human beings. I feel entitled to point out, though, that the risen dead do not make war against one another, as the living do, nor do they employ violence against one another in their homes and workplaces. Their treatment of the living might seem to be harsh, but that is because you do have not reached the understanding I am ambitious to communicate to you. In fact, it is with respect to the living that the reanimated dead exercise the greatest kindness of all—which is to say that they do their utmost to relieve them of the harsher burdens of preparatory life. What you see as mere murder, the dead see as a first stage of metamorphosis, and the sole emotion that their consciousness entertains is pity for their fellows who have not yet discovered their true destiny. If they are sometimes a trifle precipitate in recruiting others to their ranks, it is only because they are anxious to do good. They know that they would obtain the informed consent of their recruits, if they had the time to educate them fully—but they are not as well-equipped to be educators as men of your sort are, and inevitably prefer to conduct themselves expeditiously."

The rhetoric of this speech was so florid, in spite of its lack of tonal inflection, that Melkarth had to remind himself that he was talking to a djinni—a malicious prince of liars—and not a fellow diplomat. Unfortunately, his momentary pause left an opportunity open for his subordinates.

"Our *true* destiny, as human beings," Zainul Abedin put in, "is the destiny incorporated into our being by our creator, the One True God—which is to undergo a metamorphosis of a very different sort, so that our souls may spend eternity in paradise. No true believer would ever consent to become a slave of Evil."

"It is true, alas, that your creator cheated you of much of your potential, Zainul Abedin," Cimejez said—and this time, the djinni's voice did take on a very slight inflection, subtly suggestive of sadness. "When you consider that He was more generous in his treatment of the humble scarab, you are surely entitled to feel resentful of that, and perhaps it is a measure of your humility and meek acceptance, rather than your ignorance, that you refrain from such resentment. I am proud to be the bearer of glad tidings, in telling you that you need no longer be dependent on the generosity of your creator, for you have now met your potential re-creator. You have the opportunity now to become something better than your God made you: to defy death and scorn the faint, feeble and false hope of eternal paradise."

"An opportunity, my lord?" Melkarth replied, having made a curt sign to Zainul Abedin to be silent. "Do you mean that we, unlike our soldiers and our servants, will be given a choice? Does it mean that we shall not be summarily slaughtered, as our companions were?"

Cimejez leaned forward on his throne, whose unforgiving angles would surely have made it very uncomfortable for a living being to sit upon. He supported himself on his elbow, in a pose suggestive of casual indolence, and stared Melkarth in the face with his uncanny black eyes. "If I intended you to be hastened to metamorphosis, my dear wise man," the Lord of the Dead said, "then you would have been killed when your erstwhile companions were killed. Why else would you have been brought here alive but to give you a choice? Have you not seen that there are hundreds of the living among us, who have consented to remain in that state for a little longer in order that they might serve us in ways that the living find easier than the dead? Do you not understand that they will choose their own times of metamorphosis, when they are ready, and that you have already been granted the same privilege? There are no slaves of any sort in the Land of the Dead, nor is there any principle of Evil here."

"Forgive me for saying so, my lord," Melkarth retorted, "but the servant girls you gave us seem to be under some kind of magic spell, which has made them forget their past. I cannot believe that they came here of their own free will, any more than I did, and I cannot believe that they remain here by choice, any more than I intend to do."

"You do not understand, as yet, what choice you have to make," Cimejez replied. Once again, his voice was devoid of all inflection, but Melkarth could not help but read the statement as a sinister threat.

"And exactly how, my lord," Melkarth asked, trying to keep his own tone perfectly level, "do you propose to help us to understand?"

Cimejez shook his strangely slender but massive head, as if he were attempting, unsuccessfully, to feign sorrow. "You are afraid, Melkarth," the Lord of Death said. "You may be forgiven for that. I was eager to see you because I wanted to reassure you that you will not be subjected to any mistreatment. It is true, I admit, that some among the living are too stupid to understand what I am doing here, and have little or nothing to contribute to my cause. In those cases, for purely merciful reasons, I do assist them to forget their former lives, and adapt them carefully to their new duties—by means that you would consider magical, although it is an art that any thinking mind might learn and master. I would be very reluctant to treat you and your companions in the same fashion, though, for I am very curious to be informed as of the progress the world of men has made since I have been away, and I believe that you are men who can do that. I would like you to be my viziers, as you were viziers in Karbala, to assist in my education and give me sound advice. Will you do that, Melkarth, if I can convince you that it is the best thing to do?"

"If the four of us refuse, my lord," Melkarth countered, "will you release us, and give us the means to return to Karbala, alive and well?"

"I will," said the Lord of the Dead, but hastened to add: "if that is still your desire in seven days' time. I must have time, must I not, to educate you? You are wise men, not superstitious fools, and aristocrats, not common human clay. You have the power of understanding, in which the capacity for rational decision is based. You will concede me seven days, will you not, for the purpose of rational persuasion?"

Melkarth knew that he had been maneuvered into a trap, but he also knew that there was no way out of it. He was not in a position to make demands—but he was free to make requests. "I am perfectly willing to grant you seven days, Lord Cimejez," he said, smoothly, "for I am very interested to know what is happening here, and why. I shall be glad to have the opportunity to study your city, your subjects, and your noble self. I shall be glad to listen to everything you have to tell me—but I must ask two favors in return."

The way in which he had framed this statement left Cimejez little alternative but to ask what those two favors might be—which the archetype of the animated dead obligingly did.

"Firstly," said Melkarth, who knew that it was good strategy to begin with something innocuous, "We should like to have our own servants brought to our apartments, for they are like sons to us; we owe them a duty of protection, and they understand our needs."

"Granted," said Cimejez. "Secondly?"

"We ask that we might be allowed to refrain, during this period of seven days, from answering any questions of yours that would make us guilty of treason against our kingdom, our species or the One True God. If, once we understand you better, our loyalties have shifted significantly, we will doubtless answer you fully thereafter, but in the meantime...." He deliberately left the sentence incomplete.

"That is an awkward request," Cimejez observed, calmly, "for I am exceedingly eager to know as much as possible, as soon as possible, about the greater world, and I have to admit that I have been direly disappointed by the ignorance of the living captives that my armies have so far gathered. The huge increase in human numbers does not seem to have resulted in a similar increase in the general level of education. I admire loyalty, though, and I admit that I shall need to win yours if you are to be if use to me, so I agree. Until you are willing to answer my questions of your own free will, I shall not press for answers. In the meantime, I shall be content to answer yours."

Melkarth could sense his colleagues' palpable relief, and their gratitude to him for winning this concession, although he had his private reservations about the value of his victory. "Thank you, my lord," he said.

"Withdraw now," said Cimejez. "I have other business to attend to, and you are doubtless in need of rest—but be sure that I shall summon you again before very long. Hold yourself ready, if you please. Tomorrow night, by the way, there will be an entertainment here, to which you are all invited. You will find it instructive as well as amusing."

That took Melkarth slightly by surprise, but he was quick to improvise a reply. "Ah yes," he said. "I noticed the captives that arrived at the city gate a little before us, and recognized them as a company of performers, headed by a famous acrobat. They have graced many of the courts of Araby and Persia, and will do credit to yours."

For the first time, Cimejez seemed somewhat at a loss. "What is an acrobat?" the djinni asked.

"A gymnast, my lord," Melkarth replied, suppressing a smile— but he did not want to annoy the djinni, so he only paused momentarily before adding: "The troupe also includes some excellent dancers. I think you will find much to admire in their artistry—and they will allow you a precious insight into the progress that the world of men has made in the thousand years that you have been away."

Cimejez obviously knew what a dancer was, and he nodded. "Quite so," he said. "Thank you, Melkarth—I ought, indeed, to add as many living performers to the entertainment as is practicable, and I shall instruct Tahir to search for musicians, dancers and performers of every other sort among the recent captives. It will make an interesting exercise in comparison. I knew that you would be a useful addition to my court."

"You are very welcome, my lord," said Melkarth. "There is certainly no treason in recommending human arts of that sort to your consideration."

5.

Once they had returned to their quarters, Zainul Abedin was quick to observe—rather ambivalently—that Melkarth had taken a very friendly tone with the Lord of the Dead.

"Indeed I did," Melkarth said, "and I hope to keep him as amiable as possible for as long as possible. If I can find ways to amuse him harmlessly, I might be able to distract him from menacing us with inducements to satisfy his curiosity that we would find hard to resist."

"And you really hope to do that with acrobats and dancing-girls?" said Alkadi al Medoun, skeptically.

"Yes I do," Melkarth said. "As you have observed yourself, the Land of the Dead has no rich heritage, artistically speaking. Its architecture and furniture are crude, its painting primitive. Cimejez did not appear to know the meaning of the words *acrobat* and *gymnast*. Even though he was quick to emphasize that he knows what music is, and what dancing is, I cannot believe that the reanimated dead have any skill in such pursuits, or that the living servants whose memories he has found it prudent to suppress have retained any such talents. Although I cannot help thinking of him as *he*, Cimejez is sexless, so I suppose we cannot hope that the notorious Zelome will have the same effect on him as she has on human rulers and their lascivious courtiers, but djinn might not be incapable of appreciating the grace and beauty of movement of which authentic flesh is capable. In the final analysis, we must entertain our captor in some fashion, if we are to persuade him to let us live for a while longer, and I would rather entertain him harmlessly than instruct him in more practical arts."

"It might buy us a little time," Dwidar al Saad agreed. "In our situation, every minute of every day is precious."

"Perhaps more precious than we know," Melkarth said, in a low voice. "Half a hundred warriors from the legion of the dead overwhelmed our little caravan easily enough, and a similar party obviously had no difficulty in capturing a troupe of traveling performers—but the Emirates are alerted now, and will be mustering their own armies. The risen dead are difficult to kill again, it seems, but they are not invulnerable; deprived of the use of their legs, let alone of their heads, they become impotent. Our armies are far better equipped now than any army of a thousand years ago; we have chariots, couched lances, armored elephants and all manner of catapults and siege-engines. I believe that we might win this war, if our human masters can only combine their forces and strike swiftly, with a determined will. Time, in that context, might indeed be precious—and I intend to win as much as I can from our host while he is still disposed to pretend to be charming and generous."

The first of his requests was granted as he was speaking; Tahir brought Hamdan, Syed and Elaq back from the prison to which they had been taken. The three servants were exceedingly glad to be returned to the masters they knew, and were very enthusiastic to tell Melkarth everything they had seen and learned.

"At present," Hamdan reported, "there are only a few more that ten times ten living prisoners in the compound, most of them herdsmen. They will not be any use as rebels, but there are many who are avid to escape, and cunning enough to plan attempts that have some chance of success. One man with a brace of stolen camels and a good supply of water might succeed in reaching the shore of the Red Sea to spread the news of what is happening here and rouse resistance to it."

"That is excellent news," Melkarth said.

"May I make my own plans, my lord, in case an opportunity should arise?" Hamdan asked.

"You may," Melkarth told him. "You have my blessing—and if Tahir can be persuaded to brings us writing materials, I shall give you a warrant that will guarantee your welcome among the living and entitle you to a substantial reward."

When he returned to his colleagues, however, he was careful to moderate his excitement. "We must remember that we are dealing with a powerful djinni," he said. "He may be ignorant of the present state of the world, but he certainly does not seem to be stupid. He will try to trick us, as we shall try to trick him, and we must be on our guard."

He had cause to remember this the following morning, when he was summoned to a second audience with Cimejez, this time alone.

"Have you slept and eaten well, Melkarth?" the Lord of the Dead enquired, smoothly.

"Yes, my lord, I have," Melkarth replied. He refrained from adding the observation that the food supplies looted from the captured caravans were already deteriorating, as well as being in short supply, in case it set the wrong tone for the interview.

"I am glad to hear it," Cimejez replied. "A man who is well rested is a man with a clear mind, and I need you to maintain a clear mind. As soon as you are properly informed, I believe that you will see quite clearly where your true interests lie. You will, in the end, be glad to perform the functions I request of you, and I hope to have your company, as a living man, for some years to come. In the work of the intellect, even more than the work of the flesh, there are significant tasks in which the living are more accomplished than the dead—and in matters of intellectual entertainment, the wisest of the living may have much to offer the wisest of the djinn."

Melkarth took this for flattery—to which, as a diplomat, he was thoroughly accustomed. "I fear that you might be underestimating your task of persuasion, my lord," he said, mildly. "In our legendary lore, the man who is credited with greater wisdom than any other who has ever lived is the Suleiman who is said to have set his Seal upon the various prisons to which the djinn of Araby were confined a thousand years ago. We think of him as a great prophet and a hero for having achieved that. I must confess, now that I am in your august presence, that I find you a somewhat fearsome sight, and that I could not be displeased were some similar hero to return you to your prison forthwith."

Cimejez did not seem in the least angry, nor did he laugh. Perhaps, Melkarth thought, the Lords of Death were not capable of anger, or of laughter. "Suleiman was no wise man, but a great fool," the skull-faced giant informed him, flatly. "Azazel made him a false promise, which he could not recognize as a lie. Azazel offered Suleiman immortality in the flesh in return for his assistance in duping the Lords of Death. Suleiman was then besotted with the Queen of Sheba—another of Azazel's instruments—and was deluded into believing that the perpetuation of his fleshy appetites and frailties was not only possible but desirable. He did as the traitor asked, but his reward was meager."

"Why did Azazel want to destroy you?" Melkarth asked, curiously. "Our legendary lore claims that he was one of you, and the most powerful of you, until he took it into his head to attempt your destruction."

"That is probably Suleiman's testimony," Cimejez replied, "and it is false in every respect. Azazel was not one of our close company, nor was he more powerful than us, nor did he desire to destroy us. He could not destroy us, in fact, for mortality is as impossible to us as immortality is to your species. He wanted to delay us in extending the Empire of Death throughout the world, though, because he preferred to play a different game with human clay."

"I had heard that you were fond of games, my lord," Melkarth remarked. "All of this is merely a game to you, then—and it brings you into conflict with your fellow djinn as well as living men."

"How could it be anything else but a game?" the Lord of Death countered. "Even living humans, who are mere ephemera, used to play games to while away the time, in the days when we ruled the Land of the Dead before. Do they still?"

"They do, my lord," Melkarth conceded.

"Were humans capable of immortality, as we are," Cimejez went on, "they would have eternity to while away, and would have no alternative but to invent games to make the experience interesting. Only the perpetual threat of irreparable death creates and supports the illusion that there any kind of intrinsic purpose in the mere fact of existence. The wise among you, at least, ought to be able to see that attempts to defy and deny that irreparable death are, in essence, merely a game played in earnest."

"The observation has been made, my lord," Melkarth conceded. "But the risen dead who serve as your instruments are not immortal either, if I read their situation right. They still exist under the threat of permanent extinction. They are only pieces in your game, not players."

"That is true," Cimejez said. "Humans, alive or reanimate, cannot presently design games that extend across the generations—but you, Melkarth of Karbala, will at least have the privilege of choosing the game in which you are to function as a piece, and I hope and trust that you will make a wise choice."

"I'm sure I shall," Melkarth replied, feigning confidence although he could not help but find the other's blithe confidence every bit as intimidating as his nightmarish appearance. "I still cannot see, though, how you hope to persuade us that we ought to join your cause willingly and wholeheartedly?"

"You shall see soon enough," Cimejez told him. "Thank you, by the way, for recommending that I search among my captives for performers worthy of taking part in tonight's entertainment. Tahir has found several, and I shall be very interested to see how your living dancers compare with mine."

Melkarth did not know why the djinni had changed the subject, and he hesitated over his reply. He could not help glancing swiftly around the throne-room, at the strange wall-paintings and their blasphemous depictions of chimerical creatures.

"I have heard that your arts of decoration are now somewhat in advance of ours," Cimejez commented. "I have heard mention of Byzantium, Baghdad and ancient Babylon."

"The arts of construction and decoration have made some progress while you have been asleep or imprisoned, my lord," Melkarth said. "The progress has not been smooth, alas—Babylon is gone, and Athens but a shadow of its former glory—but the makers of present-day cities have inherited a rich knowledge of the possibilities of design."

"I am delighted to hear it," Cimejez replied. "Has the same progress been reflected in the purer arts? Have they been much improved, even without aesthetically-sophisticated djinn to assist in their cultivation?"

Melkarth hesitated again, not sure where the conversation was leading. "If you are referring to the arts of mathematics, music and dance, my lord," he said, "I believe that we have made good progress, as we have in painting, sculpture, oratory, song, lyric and epic poetry, history and drama."

"The dead do not speak or sing as the living do," Cimejez said, "nor do they calculate or write, although the djinn are well aware of the advantages that history has over legend, and calculation over estimation. The dead do not see as the living do, either, for their eyes have undergone metamorphosis along with the rest of their reanimated flesh—but movement is more elementary than sight, and their black hearts still beat with some sort of fundamental rhythm."

"For which reason," Melkarth said, agreeably "they evidently appreciate music and dance more fully than the other arts I mentioned—and the Lords of the Dead, having the same material form as their artifacts, are equally disposed to favor music and the dance over other arts. To the extent that you and I have aesthetic perceptions in common—or aesthetic perceptions that overlap—they pertain to music and movement."

"That is what I was trying to communicate," said Cimejez, nodding his strange head in satisfaction. "Thank you for putting it so neatly."

"I must admit, though, my lord," Melkarth said, carefully, "that I cannot believe that djinn and the dead can take as much *pleasure* in music and dance as the living do."

"Agreed," said Cimejez, mildly. "Pleasure is a prerogative of the living, which djinn and the dead believe to be greatly over-rated. In the estimation of the reanimated dead, there is a certain cruel perversity in pleasure. They—and I—have a purer and more refined notion of beauty, quality and value."

"Perhaps they—and you—do," Melkarth conceded, "in the limited sense that ambulant skeletons are purer for the lack of flesh, and more refined for the transparency of that which remains. For myself, I find no lack of purity and refinement in Athenian sculpture and drama, or the fine architecture of Byzantium, not to mention the oratory of Rome—and I have a particular fondness for the dancing-girls of Karbala, Baghdad and Isfahan; I can assure you that there is no lack of refinement there. Our living dancers know what use to make of their soft, vibrant flesh in responding to the rhythms of our musical instruments."

"I had deduced as much from your observations last evening," Cimejez said. "Would you, by any chance, be interested in making a wager?"

"A wager, my lord?" Melkarth echoed, warily. "What kind of wager?"

"You have kindly invited me—challenged me, one might almost say—to make tonight's planned entertainment into a kind of competition, in which living performers will be matched against dead ones. I fear that I cannot provide any acrobats, and will have to be content to be educated by whatever it is that they do, but I can provide musicians and dancers—and I wondered if, perhaps, you might be interested in wagering on the outcome of their comparison with the living?"

Melkarth had not the slightest doubt that he was being lured into some kind of trap, and knew that he had to be exceedingly careful—but he remembered, too, that it was by means of a wager of some sort that Suleiman the Magnificent had obtained the means or the opportunity to bind the djinn. Opinions seemed to differ as to whether Azazel had been the instigator of the deception or its victim, but the ultimate result had certainly been the banishment from the world of the Lords of the Dead.

"I shall, of course, be very interested to hear the music of the dead, and to see the dead dance," Melkarth said, treading very softly indeed. "I shall take pleasure, too, in introducing you to the talents of Zelome, whose dancing I have been privileged to see, even though I cannot be as confident that I can educate you in the aesthetic value of life as you seem to be that you can educate me in the aesthetic value of death. Since you and I perceive things so very differently and might both be unable to understand or appreciate what the other has to show us, I do not see how the outcome of any competition could be decided. Where could we find a neutral jury?"

"That is a problem, I admit," Cimejez conceded. "And it is, of course, impossible to make a wager without agreeing a jury. I am, however, quite confident that beings of my kind are the only ones who understand the true nature and artistry of dance—and that beings of your kind, however differently they might see and feel things, would appreciate the superiority of our understanding, were they to see the dance of death."

Melkarth was a well-traveled man, who had begun his life in the Gothic kingdom, in which Christendom was firmly rooted. He knew what the phrase "dance of death" signified in that context: it referred to images of a sort also called the *danse macabre*, in which personalized Death appeared in the symbolic form of a skeleton—a skeleton not so very unlike Lord Cimejez, save for the latter's gloss of artificial flesh—leading a train of dancers, each one holding the hand of the next. Melkarth had every reason to think, though, that Cimejez had no knowledge at all of that tradition in art, and must mean something quite different by the phrase.

The symbolism of the *danse macabre*, Melkarth understood, was intended to stress the ultimate irrelevance of matters of human social differences in the context of eternity. The artists who painted such dances always took care to include a wide range of social types in Death's train: men and women; young and old; rich and poor; knights and priests; merchants and soldiers; scholars and servingmaids. In the petty empires of the Lords of the Dead, it seemed, there were no apparent social distinctions other than the one that separated the living and the dead, so there could be no need there for the symbolism of the *danse macabre*. What, then, did Cimejez mean by "the dance of death"?

On the other hand, Melkarth thought, Cimejez could have not the slightest notion of what Melkarth and other living men might perceive in Zelome's dancing. Was it conceivable, he wondered, that living men could possibly prefer *any* "dance of death" to Zelome's dance of life?

"If you are offering to allow a living jury to decide the contest," Melkarth said, slowly, "then I might indeed be interested in a wager—but what stakes did you have in mind?"

"The obvious ones, of course," Cimejez said. "You are, perhaps understandably, reluctant to offer me your wholehearted collaboration in my enterprise. You do not want to answer my questions, because you think that you might be committing treason by doing so. I, on the other hand, would dearly like to have your wholehearted commitment to my cause, and to have you answer all my questions freely. Powerful as I am, I cannot compel your intellectual cooperation in the same way that I can compel the physical cooperation of mere servants—and that is why I am willing to make a wager with you. If you win, you and your three companions may go free, and your three servants too, if you wish. You may have camels, and such food supplies as we can spare. If you lose, then you must abandon your objections to assisting me, and swear wholehearted allegiance. You must tell me everything I need and desire to know, and help me formulate my plans. I think that the balance of the stakes is more than fair, in the present circumstances."

"Let us be quite clear as to the parameters of the wager," Melkarth said. "Zelome is to compete against a single dancer nominated by you, before a living jury. If the jury prefers Zelome's dance, then you will let the seven of us go—and Zelome too—with the means to reach the coast of the Red Sea."

"You seem to be increasing the stakes slightly," Cimejez observed, "But yes, those are the terms of the suggested wager. They are better, I can assure you, than the terms of the wager that Suleiman made with Azazel—although, whether I win or lose, I shall not turn traitor to my own kind, as Azazel was only too anxious to do."

Melkarth though it best not to rise to that bait. "Who will be appointed to the jury, my lord?" he asked.

"Would you be content to have your former servants serve in that capacity, along with four fellows that they may select from the company of captives presently held in the city? Seven men ought to suffice, don't you think?"

"Seven would be more than adequate, my lord," Melkarth conceded, "but I would prefer three men in whom I have confidence. Since you have offered me Hamdan, Syed and Elaq, why not let those three do the job?"

"I think you might be relying on their loyalty as much as their innate prejudice," Cimejez said. "I should like a certain balance, but I will not insist on their being outnumbered. Will you accept a six-man jury?"

"I will," Melkarth said, "if you are still willing to let Hamdan pick the other three members from the pool of prisoners—and provided that the jury reaches a unanimous verdict."

"You drive a hard bargain," Cimejez said, "but I cannot blame you for that. It is agreed. Should the jury decide unanimously in favor of your Zelome, I shall do everything possible to facilitate your return to the lands of the living. Indeed, I will add the three other members of the jury to your company, if you think that will relieve them of any undue pressure to decide in my favor. Should the jury decide unanimously in favor of my dancer, though, you will serve me exactly as I desire, both before and after your death, as cleverly and as loyally as you have served any living emir."

This seemed to Melkarth to be a very good bargain, given that he was already a captive, helpless to escape or resist—and for that very reason, he was exceedingly suspicious of it. But what other option did he have? What other hope did he have? He was already among the dead, and might very soon be dead himself. What, in the final analysis, could he possibly lose by making the wager…except, perhaps, the ever-fickle favor of the One True God? "You are very generous, my lord," he said, quietly. "I accept."

"Djinn do not reckon generosity in quite the same terms as the living," Cimejez told him, "but I am glad that you are satisfied with your cleverness. I shall send your dancing girl to your apartments, so that you can help her to prepare for the contest. In the meantime, I shall make arrangements for your servants to select the other members of their jury, and I shall summon an appropriate audience for the evening's entertainment."

6.

When Melkarth told his companions about the wager he had made, they were immediately anxious that it might be a trap into which he had fallen, but they agreed with him that it was likely to be the best bargain that could possibly be made on their behalf. The three servants were even more elated, and thanked Melkarth profusely for his efforts on their behalf.

"I made no specific promises on anyone else's behalf," Melkarth pointed out. "Even if I lose the wager, by some unimaginable trick of fate, I am the only one who will be obliged to lend his cooperation to Cimejez. The rest of you may keep your consciences clear—and you are unlikely to be put under undue pressure to tell him what you know, since none of you know anything significant that I do not."

Zainul Abedin frowned at this, but held his tongue, judging that it was not a good time to boast loudly about his supposed arcane knowledge.

Zelome was brought to the viziers' quarters in order that she might be instructed as to her role, while Hamdan, Syed, and Elaq returned to the prison to select three further jurors and explain to them what they ought to do.

Zelome had danced at least once in each of the courts of the northern Emirates, and was thus very experienced in her art, although she was not yet twenty years old.

"Your first task is to entrance and delight the six jurors," Melkarth told her, "but I think we may take it for granted that six healthy lads will have no difficulty whatsoever falling under your spell. There is, however, a greater task that you need to undertake, if it is humanly possibly, and that is to entrance Cimejez. Our first duty is to escape from this place, if we can, but we have a higher one. We ought not to be content with serving our own individual interests, but must do our utmost to serve as champions of life against death. Our ultimate goal is to demonstrate to this so-called Lord of the Dead that he is aspiring to the wrong sort of empire, and would do better to abandon his mad quest, allowing the living to live—and, eventually, to die—after their own God-given fashion. You must, therefore, do your very best to dance as no living human has ever danced before: to achieve a standard of perfection that no one in that desolate throne-room, whether living or dead, had previously imagined possible. It would be absurd for me to ask you whether you can do that, but I can ask you whether you will try."

"Yes, master," the dancer replied, "I will certainly try."

"That is what I wanted to hear," Melkarth told her. "You have only to do your best. If you cannot win this wager for me, then it is unwinnable. Cimejez must think that it is unwinnable, or he would not have made the offer—but we must hope, and believe, that we can prove him wrong. He has been defeated before, and put to sleep for a thousand years, so we may be confident that it can be done again, if only we can find the way."

"Do you know anything about the dancer who will be my rival?" Zelome asked. "Will it be one of the skull-faces?"

"I presume so," Melkarth said, "but that was not specified; all that I know for sure is that your rival will be one of the risen dead."

"I have heard that serpentine lamias are very fine dancers," the girl said, dubiously. "I heard, too, that one of the Emir of Luvah's courtiers was once visited in his dreams by a dancing succubus, which charmed the vital fluids from his body. I am not afraid of any skull-face—but before I came here, I understood the dead who linger on Earth to be delicate wraiths. If I were matched against a wraith who was a famous dancer while she was alive, and is now even lighter on her feet...."

"Don't think about that," Melkarth told her. "The wager pits the dance of life against the dance of death; as you embody and represent life, your rival will embody and represent death. I doubt that Cimejez would pick a champion on the grounds that its flesh, in its former ensouled state, was able to please a human audience—but if he does, it will not be to your disadvantage."

"I shall follow your advice and not think about it," Zelome said, resolutely. "I am a dancer through and through; I have only to be what I am—and could not, in any case, attempt to be anything else. It would, as you say, be absurd for me to claim that I can dance well enough to charm the dead, but the dream that has guided me throughout my life and career is that of dancing more beautifully than anyone has ever danced before, and I truly believe that I am as well-equipped as I shall ever be to make the attempt."

"Excellent," said Melkarth.

He was not so pleased by the musicians who had been captured along with Zelome, whose skills proved to be very ordinary indeed when he examined them, but Zelome told him that they would be adequate to her needs. She picked out a zither-player, a cymbalist and a drummer, and Melkarth did his best to explain the importance of their task in a way that might bring the best out of them.

"Let us all do what we can to show these reanimated corpses what it means to be alive," he said to the four of them, before they set off to practice and rehearse. "Let us all demonstrate our passionate love of life, and remind the forgetful skull-faces what it is they have lost. Let us reintroduce these paradoxical beings to the bittersweetness of honest regret."

Melkarth asked Tahir to allow the dancer to examine all the costumes looted from various caravans, in order that she might find the one most appropriate to her purpose. He agreed to do that.

"Do you really believe," said Zainul Abedin, when Zelome and the instrumentalists had gone "that this Prince of Liars will honor his bargain? Surely he is toying with you, Melkarth."

"Perhaps he is," Melkarth admitted. "If he is indeed a Prince of Liars, who will simply break his word, then we are lost—but I do not believe that he is. I believe that he really is insanely over-confident, and insanely fond of gaming. What choice do I have but to believe that? What other opportunity can I possibly exploit? The djinn have been away from these lands for a thousand years. Unless we can rediscover the secret of Suleiman's Seal within seven days—of which only six now remain—the only advantage we have is the djinns' evident ignorance of the progress that has been made while they were asleep."

7.

Cimejez had assembled a huge audience for the contest, which his overseers had distributed around the great hall of his palace. All the living prisoners recently taken by his army had been brought from their cells, but they were numbered no more than a hundred and twenty. There were at least four hundred skull-faced workmen and soldiers packed into the margins of the room, and the audience was further augmented by fifty of the djinni's living servants and forty of the strange chimeras with animal heads. All of these watchers were standing, and so were the six members of the jury, who were situated to the left of Cimejez's throne. To the right of the throne, however, five chairs had been set in a line, four of which were reserved for the diplomats from Karbala. The fifth remained empty even when the audience was fully assembled.

"You are the challenger here," Cimejez said to Melkarth. "Is it agreeable to you that your champion should take the first turn?"

"Indeed it is," Melkarth replied. To Zelome, he added: "Make the living proud and dead ashamed of their relative conditions."

Zelome went to her work with a will. The musicians began to play, and she strode proudly into the arena, poised to perform the legendary Dance of the Seven Veils.

Melkarth had seen the dance before, but he knew that the six jurors would never have had the opportunity to see it; it was a performance usually limited to the sight of men of great distinction. Vulgar rumor sometimes represented the dance in question as a mere strip-tease, intended to tantalize with a promise of nudity that was finally, if momentarily, fulfilled, but Melkarth understood how much more than that it really was. He knew that each of the seven veils had its own symbolism, and that each ritual removal was part of a measured progress from misery to ecstasy. He understood that each garment represented one of the vicissitudes of common misfortune, and that as each one was discarded, the dancer advanced towards a uniquely joyous freedom: the epitome of life's rewards. It was, he thought, a perfect choice for the task in hand.

The zither-player, the cymbalist and the drummer had all played the music of the Dance of the Seven Veils before, albeit for performances of a slightly less exalted nature, and it was sufficiently unchallenging to be well within their artistic compass. They not only contrived to get the notes in the right order, but also to inject a measure of assistant feeling into them. As the dance unfolded, Zelome contrived to communicate some of her own inspiration to them, so that they improved by degrees as the performance progressed.

The first potential curse capable of afflicting life, according to the Dance of the Seven Veils, was hunger—which, for the purpose of the dance, included and subsumed thirst. The first phase of Zelome's interpretation was, therefore, the embodiment in body-language of the most fundamental of appetites: the one that shapes the successful quest of a new-born infant for a mother's milk and a mother's love. The first phase of the dance ended with the symbolic satisfaction of that craving.

The second potential curse capable of spoiling life, according to the dance, was cold, so the second phase of Zelome's version was the embodiment in movement of the need for clothing and shelter, and of its eventual achievement. The third potential curse was disease—which, for the purpose of the dance, also embraced injury—so the third phase of the performance comprised a symbolic celebration of the power of the body to heal itself, and the wisdom of physicians. The fourth curse was loneliness, and the fourth phase of the dance was shaped as a hymn of praise to society and amity, and the productive rewards of co-operative labor. The fifth curse was loss, and Zelome lent a particular emphasis to that particular movement within the whole, making a very conspicuous demonstration of the agony of grief, which gave way by slow and stately degrees to the triumph of resolution and the recognition of all the legacies that the dead, in ordinary human society, conveyed to the living.

By this time, the crescendo of music and movement was becoming almost unbearable in its suspense—or so Melkarth judged, even though he had not yet surrendered himself wholly to the performance, and it did not require overmuch effort to direct his eyes away from the dancer in the enter of the room, in order to study the jury, the crowd, and Cimejez himself.

The jury left no possible doubt as to their captivation; they were completely under Zelome's spell. The reanimated dead, on the other hand, seemed quite indifferent and utterly impassive—but Melkarth was delighted to observe that the same was not true of the Lord of the Dead's living minions, whether their heads were human or animal. They were moving their bodies to the rhythm of the dance in spite of the fact that they were crowded so close together, and their eyes were hypnotized.

They, at least, are being forced to remember, Melkarth thought. *Whatever black spells Cimejez has cast on the recalcitrant among them, and whatever sophistry he has employed upon the tractable, it is not proof against such innocent, God-given magic as this. There, at least, seeds of rebellion have been sown, and an urge to escape. If only a few of those seeds come to fruition, we have done good work here today. It would be better, though, if the risen dead could be moved in their turn.*

As for the Lord of the Dead himself, Cimejez did not seem quite as unmoved as his mute subjects—but it was impossible for Melkarth to guess exactly what the emotion was that seemed to be disturbing the contours of his transparent cheeks.

The sixth potential curse capable of afflicting human life, according to the Dance of the Seven Veils, was childlessness, so the sixth phase of Zelome's extravaganza was a celebration of sexual love, marriage and parenthood. It was even longer than the fifth, although it posed the greatest challenge so far to Zelome's genius, given that she was herself too young ever to have suffered the agonies of frustration that she had to demonstrate. Melkarth was very keenly aware, however, that the sixth phase—and, indeed, all six of the preliminary phases calculated in their sum—was merely a prelude to the seventh.

Thus far, Melkarth had been watching with the critical eye of a connoisseur in spite of Zelome's intention to enchant him and his own desire to be incapable, in the end, of dissolving his intellect in the rapture of the dance. He found little to criticize, though. It was easy enough to see that Zelome had not been exhaustively trained in the conventional devices of Arab dancing, but it was equally obvious that her spontaneity and exuberance more than made up for that omission. She was authentically gifted, and her appeal to the emotions of her audience was no less powerful because it lacked a certain refinement and sophistication. Whatever imperfection remained in the playing of her accompanists was easily ignored; the dancer was the only centre of attention, the sole contestant. By the time the sixth veil was shed, the living members of the audience were following her with their eyes, utterly captivated by her every movement. Even the black eyes of the dead were riveted to her person, in spite of the apparent indifference of their attitude. They must have been reminded of life, if they were still capable of memory, even if the echo were too faint, as yet, to make them regret its loss.

It was, Melkarth supposed, entirely possible that the risen dead literally *could not* care—but the mere fact that had been raised to further action, and equipped with motive force of some kind, implied that they ought to have the capacity to respond to the art of the dance; the problem was to reach and activate that potential. There was still one phase of the dance to be completed, and Melkarth knew that whatever hope he had of capturing the black hearts of the skull-faces rested on that last phase, but he could not be at all certain how the dead would respond to it. Even so, he dared to hope.

The final curse afflicting human life, according to the Dance of the Seven Veils, was the awareness of the inevitability of death—not death itself, but the consciousness, fear and horror of personal extinction, and its corollary sense of the futility of all endeavor. The final act of Zelome's drama had to consist of a heroic defense of the meaning of life in the face of inevitable death: of trust in God's bounty and purpose, of delight in creative achievement, and of pride in the fact that, although a body and mind might be annihilated, the legacy of their attainments could not.

Zelome danced that final phase as well as Melkarth could possibly have wished. The last and longest phase of the dancing-girl's masterpiece was, in essence, a celebration of the joy and meaning of dance itself, and its conclusion was an affirmation of the fact that life was, in essence, a kind of dance, and therefore might fabricated, if it were only lived well, out of joy and meaning.

The consummation and climax of the final phase was the removal of the final veil: the revelation of the human being beneath, utterly triumphant over every single one of the many indignities which cruel fate attempted perennially to heap upon her kind, but which could not in the end diminish her. Even her accompanists excelled themselves as they brought their crescendo to an end. When Zelome finally became still, the captive prisoners, all of whom were already in tears, burst into a storm of applause and acclamation, and all of the djinni's living servants joined in—but the skull-faced dead remained silent and unappreciative.

"The skull-faces do not understand," murmured Dwidar al Saad, mopping his cheeks. "Death was as inevitable for them as other men, and just as menacing, but their renewed half-life now seems to them to be the limit of possibility. They simply do not understand."

"But that does not matter," Alkadi al Medoun whispered. "They are not the judges who will decide this matter. Hamdan and his five companions are the jury, and they are ours."

"There was not one among the Lord of the Dead's living servants," Zainul Abedin opined, anxiously, "who was not captivated by the dance, and not one of the dead who was—but it should not matter. If the Lord of the Dead plays fair, it should not matter."

Melkarth, meanwhile, was looking at Cimejez, and wondering whether djinn ought to be reckoned among the living or the dead. The Lord of the Dead did seem to have been moved by the performance, though, and had joined in the applause.

When Zelome finally looked up, she sought to meet Melkarth's eyes, and he tore his gaze away from Cimejez in order to indicate his own approval with a smile and a nod. He could see that the girl was pleased with what she had done, and was glad. Cimejez beckoned to her, and then indicated with an imperious that she should take the empty seat next to Melkarth. The vizier briefly took her hand in his as she sat down, and squeezed it slightly before releasing it again, by way of congratulation.

Then the door to the throne-room was opened discreetly, and Cimejez's champion came in to take the floor.

8.

Zelome's rival was, as Melkarth had half-expected, a skull-face of sorts, but was not identical to the skull-faces in the audience. This one had less flesh than they had, although it wore a transparent robe not unlike the one the Lord of the Dead was wearing, which seemed reminiscent of loose-hanging flesh. This skull-face had no black eyes, but only empty orbits. If it had a tongue, heart or stomach, they were so transparent as to be invisible. In fact, the dancer was very similar indeed to the kind of figure routinely depicted in Western Christendom's depictions of the *danse macabre*. It resembled a skeleton whose bones were held together by magical means rather than any connective flesh. It was not an ordinary skeleton, though. It was an *imperious* skeleton, with perfect teeth set in the permanent mocking smile of the long-dead. Its transparent robe was fitted with a transparent hood, and it carried a scythe.

The zither-player, the cymbalist and the drummer had already retired from the border of the arena to join the other living captives. Their place was taken by a single drummer, also a seemingly-fleshless skeleton, but more modestly attired in a grey monkish robe. When the drummer began to caress its instrument with its slender fingers, the rhythm that was sounded was more reminiscent, in Melkarth's ears, of a military signal than a dance-beat. Indeed, as the drumbeat progressed, Melkarth recognized it as a *chamade*: the summons used by exhausted armies to call for truce and negotiation.

There were no veils in this performance, no symbolic curses and no triumphant alleviations. The dance of death had only one phase, and it had no hint of a crescendo.

It occurred to Melkarth, as he watched the skeleton begin to move to the rhythm of the *chamade*, that he had never bothered to wonder what kind of dance the *danse macabre* was, or whether it had any predetermined steps at all. The images of the dance that he had seen had been frozen moments decanted from an essentially mysterious process. Although his human eyes had always been capable of reading an implicit flow and surge into paintings and statues of dancers in action, he had never been able to do the same for the *danse macabre*. Now, for the first time in his life, he was able to see both the evolution and the revolution of the dance of death, and to understand not merely *where* it led, but how and why.

There were no phases in the dance of death, because death had no phases. There were no curses in the dance of death, because death was devoid of afflictions. There were no veils in the dance of death, because death could neither disguise nor conceal its essence. There were neither triumphs nor celebrations in the dance of death, because death was all triumph, and had no need of any celebration.

The dance of death was slow, and painstakingly measured, and eternal. The dance of death was an inexorable and inescapable summons, whose promise was more truce than release. That summons, addressed by the extinct to the exhausted, gathered in everyone and everything....except for the risen dead, who were, Melkarth realized, already dancing inside themselves, already fully aware of the true meaning and quality of their paradoxical existence.

Life, according to the symbolism of the black-clad figure's awesomely patient and painstakingly measured steps, was a struggle against fate and the terrible will of the One True God. It had its victories—which were, admittedly, the only victories conceivable—but victory was, in this context, quite irrelevant. In death, there was no strife, no violence, no hope, no *life*; if there were no victories, it was because none was needed. That was the meaning of the *chamade*, and the meaning of the dance it accompanied.

Melkarth realized, even before the skeleton had made a single circuit of the arena, that he could not win his wager, and had never had the slightest chance of winning his wager. He could not win because his opponent did not need to win; he had to lose because he was the only one who *could* lose. Cimejez had always known that, and had always known that Melkarth—heir to a thousand years of human progress as he was—could not possibly know it.

Melkarth realized, without needing to feel the slackness of her hand in his, that Zelome had come to understand it too. A few moment before, she had not been able to imagine wanting to be anything other than she was, because that was all she had ever been— she was a dancer through and through, and her life was a dance—but she wanted to be something different now. The failure had been in the capacity of her imagination, and Melkarth's; she had never seen, imagined or understood the *danse macabre*. She was watching it now, and she understood exactly how its rhythm intruded itself into the human eye, ear and mind, like a possessive djinni banishing all rival thought and sensation.

Melkarth's fellow prisoners were not applauding any longer, but they were joining in the dance. While Cimejez's living servants held back, restrained by magic, doleful in their resignation or weeping in frustration, the six jurors and their fellows from the prison shuffled forwards and surged on to the floor.

Melkarth found, not at all to his dismay, that he and his four seated companions had risen to their feet, and that they too were moving forward, intent on joining the dance—but Cimejez raised his hand abruptly, and Melkarth stopped in his tracks. Dwidar al Saad, Zainul Abedin and Alkadi al Medoun stopped too—and all four of them looked at the Lord of Death, understanding that they had different duties awaiting them, and that many years might yet pass before they were allowed to go on to the next phase of their existence.

As Melkarth met Cimejez' gaze, however, he saw, for the first time, a slight smile play upon the monstrous transparent lips, and he realized that the Lord of the Dead was himself alive, and always would be. There was a definite kindness in the djinni's expression as his gesture shifted slightly, and Melkarth felt Zelome's hand slip out of his as she continued forwards, not merely to join the dance but to take the leader's own hand and share in his authority.

That was, Melkarth understood, an act of mercy on the djinni's part; Zelome was, after all, a dancer through and through.

Now the scythe came into play. As the column of figures wound around and around, doubling back on itself again and again, the scythe offered its blade to the dancing mortals. Hand-in-hand as they were, they could offer no resistance to its seeking blade, but they did not flinch or turn away as it sliced through their flesh. They did not bleed; it was as if the scythe drank their blood to the last drop. The flesh began to shrivel on their bones, as if the dull music of the signal-drum were a consuming fire, and the transparent remnant of their tissues became a kind of molten glass tainted with lumps of black ash.

The zither-player, the cymbalist and the drummer joined in the parade with almost as much enthusiasm as Zelome herself, like true connoisseurs of rhythm. They offered themselves to the scythe as she did, glad that they would not be obliged to wait for its metamorphic gift, like the poor souls who had been forbidden to move.

"This is what the dead have to offer the living," Cimejez said, his words whispering intimately in Melkarth's ear in spite of the distance between them. "This is what might be attained, if only the living would try harder to understand the nature of the Great Crusade. Do you understand now, Melkarth, why you must commit yourself to my cause?"

"This is black magic," muttered Zainul Abedin, his voice half-strangled by some internal struggle. "The Prince of Liars has cheated us, as I feared."

Melkarth knew, however, that he had not been cheated, even though the dance of death was most certainly magic of a sort. He knew that Cimejez had played fair, even though the djinni had always known that he would win the wager, because he really did want Melkarth's consent as well as his collaboration. He wanted Melkarth *on his side*, wholeheartedly, just as Melkarth had hoped to win the dead to his cause, as well as winning his bet.

"The one thing I do not understand," Melkarth whispered, although he knew that all his companions could hear him quite clearly, "is how Suleiman ever defeated you, even with the aid of a rival djinni as clever as Azazel."

"No one defeated us," Cimejez replied, "for we cannot lose. Azazel merely made a move in an ongoing game—and now that I have seen the reward of a thousand years of human progress, I am forced to admit that it was a clever and artful move. What, I wonder, might a further thousand years of progress have produced? What might it still produce, if Zelebsel could be persuaded to curb his impatience for a while longer? But that is not your concern, my good and faithful servant. Your task, from now on, is to be a good vizier. I have every confidence that you will acquit yourself well."

Cimejez made another gesture then, and it seemed to Melkarth that an invisible bony hand caressed his forehead, with paternal affection. The pressure was gentle, but it was irresistible.

Melkarth sat down again, and his three fellows sat down with him. Filled with an infinite sensation of yearning, they were afforded the rare privilege of watching the *danse macabre* without being required to join it—and becoming, by virtue of that experience, wiser than they had been before, because they understood the strategy and the objectives of the Great Crusade.

The most remarkable thing about the continuing dance—or so it seemed to Melkarth—was the reaction of the remainder of the crowd to the performance they were watching. The skull-faces and their living collaborators did not applaud, nor did they even sway in time to the rhythm. They remained utterly silent and still. They had been reanimated to serve as warriors in the Great Crusade Against the Living; they had been given armor, and weapons, and a cause—but the motive force that impelled them to take up arms against the living was nothing like the motives that forced the living to act. Their motive force was the *danse macabre* itself, to which they made no evident response because they had no need. The dead had no need to follow the paces of the dance, or even to approve of them, for the dance was merely a reflection of their nature, like a shadow carelessly cast upon the ground.

Melkarth understood, among many other things, that he would not be a traitor to the living, no matter how the living might look upon him in future. He also understood how difficult it would be to explain that fact to all the future visitors to the City of the Dead that he would have to greet and make welcome, but he was not dismayed by the prospect. He was, after all, a diplomat.

In the meantime, he crossed his legs and watched the dance of death. It seemed to go on forever, but when it was over he had lost far less time than it took a human to be born, let alone to die.

9.

In the long, hard years of servitude that followed his arrival in the City of the Dead, Theoderic Melkarth discovered that the first curse afflicting human life is indeed hunger—which, for accounting purposes, might be taken to include and subsume thirst. He discovered, too, the scrupulous accuracy of the estimated hierarchy of needs that had ranked cold the second, disease and injury the third, loneliness the fourth, loss the fifth and childlessness the sixth. He suffered all of these afflictions in their fullest measure, but he was not allowed to die. He helped bring bountiful death to hundreds of thousands of the living, and he helped bring the greater number of those he had betrayed into the ranks of Cimejez's army, but he was not allowed the kind of release he devoutly desired, or any other kind.

Melkarth never forgot that the final curse afflicting human life is the inevitability of death itself, at least according to the Dance of the Seven Veils—but he could find little comfort in the recollection, even though the final phase of Zelome's performance was etched so deeply in his memory that he was able replay it over and over again in his restless dreams. He still knew, on an intellectual level, that the sum and climax of his existence, like that of any human being, was supposed to consist of a heroic defense of the meaning of life in the face of inevitable death—of trust in Allah's bounty and purpose, of delight in creative achievement, and of pride in the fact that, although a body and mind might be annihilated, the legacy of their attainments could not—but he was no longer able to feel it in his beating heart or in the rhythm of the blood in his veins. He had lost his faith, and could not even regret his loss. Like the djinn, he had become an enemy of the One True God: a shameless apostate.

Sometimes, though, like his master Cimejez, he could not help but wonder what another thousand years of human progress might have made of art, science, faith and the sum of ordinary human happiness, if the djinn had delayed their return.

ABOUT THE AUTHOR

BRIAN STABLEFORD was born in Yorkshire in 1948. He taught at the University of Reading for several years, but is now a full-time writer. He has written many science fiction and fantasy novels, including *The Empire of Fear*, *The Werewolves of London*, *Year Zero*, *The Curse of the Coral Bride*, and *The Stones of Camelot*. Collections of his short stories include *Sexual Chemistry: Sardonic Tales of the Genetic Revolution*, *Designer Genes: Tales of the Biotech Revolution*, and *Sheena and Other Gothic Tales*. He has written numerous nonfiction books, including *Scientific Romance in Britain, 1890-1950*, *Glorious Perversity: The Decline and Fall of Literary Decadence*, and *Science Fact and Science Fiction: An Encyclopedia*. He has contributed hundreds of biographical and critical entries to reference books, including both editions of *The Encyclopedia of Science Fiction* and several editions of the library guide, *Anatomy of Wonder*. He has also translated numerous novels from the French language, including several by the feuilletonist Paul Féval.

www.ingramcontent.com/pod-product-compliance
Lightning Source LLC
Chambersburg PA
CBHW050738250626
47155CB00005B/1829